D1827380

Introduction:

I am now sitting here in the home of the free and the land of the brave and I feel neither. Twenty years have now passed since it all happened but I am still watched, there are still cars parked outside my house, still men in rain coats leant against the lamp post. A man in a rain coat sticks out a mile here in West Beverley. They know I am no communist, but no doubt the Americans think that a man who betrayed his home country might well betray his new one, I am a serial slut so to speak. I should thank the Americans though, I would be dead without them, many people have already been killed to guard this secret, Lord knows how many over the centuries, must be at least running into the hundreds, I suppose I am lucky not to have my body piled on top of that heap of corpses.

God only knows why the secret services though put us here in Los Angeles. In the east, in New England I would be at least half home, but this is as foreign a place as any of them, a place they took off the Mexicans and tried to Yankeeise it ,but you can't change the weather or stop the Latinos crossing the border or heading here from other annexed states. I guess they thought that we would be grateful after years of bad weather in England. However to an Englishman this town is hell, the first few months you enjoy basking on the beach but after a while you miss your English cathedral city, with it's central point of a great medieval church and maybe a castle, this place is more like Birmingham, a vast sprawl with no heart or soul. It is familiar in some ways from those old silent films we use to watch back home. The street I am living in was built in those times and I will swear I have seen Buster Keaton or Harold Lloyd come out of this place in monochrome. Someone told me that Mary Pickford use to live here, there we are I couldn't even get a film star who people had still heard of.

I feel my age too now, I am nearer sixty than fifty now, where there was once muscles now only hanging flesh and the tinnitus won't let me sleep, that is part of the reason I am writing this at this hour, but it isn't the ringing in my head that gives me the bad dreams or the paranoia. When I came here Great Britain was a rival and potential enemy state, but every year since then I have seen my motherland become more and more a vassal of America. Now with India gone there is little for America to covet and anything bad for the British is bad for the Americans as well, that makes my life here less and less certain, the time cannot be too distant when they hand me over to them, then I only shudder to think what they will do to me.

There are English people here but of course I do not mix with them, whenever we hear British accents we have to change pavements sorry sidewalks. I am not saying all but some of those guys in raincoats could be from back home, now that is a chilling thought, because they loiter outside just until they get the order to come inside and kill us. I wonder if Douglas Fairbanks jnr is still working for us, sorry *them*. I guess I had better get back to sleep, I hate long introductions. It is nearly 3AM and there is no one outside at the moment, they tend not to do it at night, because one of my neighbours would report them, that is what spooked me earlier. I do not even know why I am writing this, and what I will do when it is finished, but I will put down everything I know, some of it I have pieced together from Matilda, because I was not there at sometimes, but it is all true. I would like my family to read this back home, my mother is long dead but maybe my brother, he must wonder what happened to me. The Americans have told me never to contact him because the British will know where I am. It is not that they think he would betray me but the mail would be intercepted before it got to him, when I have finished this I do not know where I will hide it, under the floorboards I think, because I am sure that this house has been searched before whilst we were out.

I must be the only Englishman in Los Angeles who doesn't want to be in the movies, not just don't want to be in one but near one. Whenever I go anywhere they ask me about films, they don't know my face so I must be a producer, director or writer, someone who can help them, get into movies, get on in life, get out of West Beverley and get a house in the hills, that's the dream of all these lab rats here.

It is October 25th and all yesterday the radio was going on about the death of Al Jolson, it had well swept President Truman and whatever he was doing off the headlines, a man who painted his face black is more important than the head of a nuclear arsenal, a man who can destroy the world. Now the radio is silent, it is all silent save my tinnitus and Matilda's snoring in the bedroom. I can't help but peer out through the curtains and look across the street. Anyway I know from the time when I read a lot that there is nothing worse than a long introduction, you just want to skip it and get to the real book. So I will close it here, if any of my family in England is reading this I am alright and miss you and home greatly,

Former Corporal Charles Simmonds, the prisoner of West Beverley, 25th October 1950.

Chapter One: A new life.

I had always known that something was going on; well it's obvious isn't it? I mean the world can't seriously be as it is. I speak as a failed writer, failed father, failed husband and failed whatever else I have tried to do in my life. What makes it worse is I know others, less educated, less resourceful and less handsome who are getting on in life. In London I had worked in a warehouse where one day my manager turned to me and asked: "How do you spell Jew? Is it JEW?"

My forehead creased since I couldn't see why he would want to use that word, maybe he was one of those anti-Semites who crowd into east end pubs, and he wanted to put a sign up saying he wouldn't employ them, that wouldn't go down too well with the owner I knew that, since some of his clients had Jewish names. "In what context, I mean what is the sentence?"

My manager leant back in his chair and replied, "Jew to unforeseen circumstances..'

I shook my head and replied, "DUE." I looked at his face; there was no sign of shame in it. That just summed it up though dear reader, here was a man who obviously had no schooling, a man whose voice was thick with a cockney accent but he was sat behind the desk giving orders and I was stood there taking them.

Maybe there was something about me that people saw that they didn't like, whatever it was it was something that I couldn't put my finger on. Maybe I was just one of those misfits who just slip through the net. Perhaps it was true what those apes in those pubs said and Jews were ruling the world, they were the puppet masters and we were all dancing at the end of their strings, if it wasn't them then it was someone. Maybe I should go to America. Maybe I should end it all. One thing was for sure, I should do something.

I was glad to have left the warehouse, I was glad to be leaving London, I was glad to be leaving my family. I was glad to driving through the Cotswolds, up hills that weren't steep enough to trouble the limousine and past picturesque yellow stone villages. The friendly wayside signs had counted down first the distance between Oxford and London and now Oxford and Worcester, marking down like some hour clock made out of cement, 60, 59, 58 and all the time Oxford got farer and farer away. I had been there before, I had even dreamt of attending university there in my stupid youth, but Worcestershire was a secret realm I knew little about. I had seen a sign up outside the Oval once saying Worcestershire, but it wasn't advertising the place, only telling Londoners that their cricket team would be visiting, I didn't even know if they were any good.

I missed my son; I would be a liar to say that I didn't. There were some problems with him, he was nearly five and had still not uttered a word, and people said they had heard him say 'hello' once but it had only been once and he had never said it again. He loved me, I knew that, maybe he was the only one who did, but he was better off without me. I had left his mother the advance my new boss had given me and a letter saying that there would be more and her job now was looking after our son and finding a new husband, a better husband, a husband who wasn't me.

Oxfordshire became a lonely place with it's desolate fields that I could only imagine people farming misery out of, you didn't have to stray far from Oxford's dreaming spires to find a bleak, uneducated world, my eyes settled on the faces of the peasants I past, as poor and down trodden as any I had seen in the east. The women all had an unattractive and unwashed look about them, in these backwoods people had been marrying their own cousins for generations, but then the women in London would look like that if you dragged them through a hedge and gave them nothing to eat for a month. The villages became scarcer until I passed a tower that looked as if it had fallen out of the world of wizards and warlocks, and then the road sank down a steep, twisting track down towards Worcestershire and it seemed to sparkle in the sunlight. It was a thrill to take my foot off the accelerator and plunge the great monster down that hill and into my new kingdom, leaving Oxford, London, and all the rest of my failures behind me.

The first village was called Broadway, like that street in New York where all you needed to do was step out onto the stage there to be met by adoration and appreciation. It's king Al Jolson was too great ever to have set foot in Europe, not since he had left it as an unwashed kid, only his pale shadow Eddie Cantor had deigned to visit London. Looking at it's name I smiled, I was though not heading to New York but in the opposite direction into a great haystack. My heart sank when I saw the village beyond the sign and the same yellow stone houses, so I had gone down that hill for no reason, the Cotswolds continued, Worcestershire was a fraud. The village was pretty enough though, it's just it was more of the same, surely God had put that hill and man had drawn that border for a reason, or maybe not after all there was no reason for anything anymore.

I thought a bit about my wife. She was more than pretty, she was beautiful, but it was one of those marriages that should never have happened. I didn't love her, not in my heart and she certainly didn't love me. If she had loved me she wouldn't have forced me to take that job in the warehouse with Dr Johnson back there, that job had been hell with me lifting up my own body weight time and time again, all the time my friend who didn't know the difference between Jew and due would just stand there and give orders, he wouldn't even lift a finger if it was panic stations, he reminded me of some of those officers in the war who seemed allergic to gunfire. Those people gave great speeches but disappeared when the battle started. I didn't know much about him but I bet that bastard had found some reason not to have gone to war, too young, too old, too ill, and too chicken.

I missed my son more than anything else, I thought it would pass, but it never did and when four years down the road the song 'Sonny Boy' became such a big hit I had to run from every place where I heard it played.

I was glad to see Worcestershire become less and less Cotwolds as I neared Evesham. It was a town that the dust passed over now, but once a huge monastery had stood there, now all that was left was a solitary bell tower. The English had gotten sick of God and all the ceremonies He demanded, maybe they had been right. Worcester itself was now only sixteen miles away, for the first time I checked my watch, I would be early, unless I got a flat or the engine packed up or something.

I had little else behind in London either. I had a family, I had met them only a year or so ago at a funeral, but I didn't know these people, cousins and aunties, the Bolsheviks could shoot them all for all I care. I had little in common with them save some physical resemblance and a surname. I passed through Pershore and glanced at it's abbey before stepping on the accelerator, now there was nothing between me and Worcester itself. I was the black sheep of the family, but like a black sheep I had done nothing to deserve it, I mean I had tried to think what I had done against my rich auntie but she distrusted and despised me. I had never asked her for money, I think maybe it was because she had hated my mother and I was the inheritor of that hate. You see my mother was one of those dear people the world has too few of, a bullshit eliminator. Sorry to use such a word, but I think it is the best phrase, and many a time my auntie opened her mouth and tried to put on airs and graces an acidic remark by my mother would shut it again. Now she was dead the mouth never closed. But that was just her, what about the others? I mean I couldn't give an excuse for all of them.

So that is what I was thinking as I headed down London Road and past it's fine houses, I was not thinking of my new job or what it's duties would be I was thinking of my family, certainly a waste of my thoughts, they always had been, maybe that's why I never got anywhere at work.

I had seen the cathedral from the countryside but as I got closer it only got more majestic more awe inspiring. This was the great palace of God Himself, built by the Normans on the ashes of it's Saxon predecessor, only God knew how men had got up to make it's huge tower, easily dwarfing the Tower of London, or anything for that matter in London. How many had fallen to their deaths from it? What suffering must have passed to build such a wonder? But it stood now forever, proof that our ancestors were greater men than we are, despite our British Empire and all that false nonsense.

As I drove closer I got the feeling that this was the real capital of England, but like me it had never gotten what was it's due. The tower looked like the helmet of a medieval knight, it's narrow windows like the dark eyes which watched everything but told nothing, like the city it was upright and honourable, the faithful city which had stood by the King, Worcester had watched all the parliaments and royalty go to London, that scoundrel place but said nothing, just waited for the scandals and wars to come before it's people came out to fight for the King again. But then maybe that was rubbish, people are the same anywhere and any city is just a mass of brick and wood to contain them, at least though London was a capital, a real capital not like Bucharest.

Ah there I have betrayed myself, not as a real writer but as a failed one. My story really started there, that is where I spent the years 1914-1917 in the Romanian capital. At this point I hear the book being put down and some of you saying: 'Yes here we have it! Another one, another one who kept his head down during the war, another one who joined the navy or got himself posted to a place where there was no fighting, another one who had it easy while our boy was out there in the hell of Flanders, and our boy was lucky to come back, or our boy came back blind, or our boy never came back at all you bastard! Well I joined up like anyone else, I was as stupid as anyone else, I lied about my age like your son did, I boasted about being one of the first to enter Berlin! The difference is I mentioned to the recruiting sergeant that I had driven a car and that I had learnt French and Latin. I never said I could speak French and Latin, but I went to a school where these things were taught. That is the difference between me and your boy and maybe that is why I am sit here writing this and your boy is dead.

In the opening days of the Great European War Bucharest was indeed the place to be. Romania was sat on the fence. There were several maps of Romania in Bucharest; the Vlachs themselves liked a map which showed Romania stretching deep into the plain of Hungary and into Serbia, a land made up of all the Romanian ancient lands. The map which everyone else had showed a country made up of the plain of Wallachia and most of Moldavia. The Austrians were sat in Bukovina and the Hungarians were in the great Dacian heart of Transylvania, Temesvar, sorry Timisoara, as we must call it now and the Maramures. That should have made things easy, and they should have waded into the conflict on our side, only the Russians were sat in eastern Moldavia, the land known as Bessarabia and that place was as Romanian as anywhere else, named after a Romanian prince. They also had a king who was as German as the Kaiser himself. That was the problem in 1914 and so we went there, I of course was a nobody, my job was to drive around Donald, he was the man who had to get Romania into the war. The mission wasn't that important in the early days, but as the war went on and we ground to a bloody halt then Romania became more and more vital. The plain of Wallachia is a prime place for growing wheat, wheat that could feed the German war machine, so we had to buy it, even though we couldn't get it out of the country, so we bought it and left it there to rot, while thousands starved. I was there when Donald paid for the wheat and I saw not thousands but millions pass his hands, often in gold. It would have been the easiest thing in the world to kill him and then make my way out of Romania; of course the whole world would have been my enemies but that much gold would have bought me a ticket to anywhere. I also knew about the negotiations, I knew more than the King of England, than Lloyd George and more importantly than the Kaiser. Donald had success at last and on the night of August 27th 1916 the Romanian army crossed the mountains to liberate their brothers from the Hungarian yoke, whatever yoke means anyway.

There I have bored you with a history lesson, but you won't read it anywhere else. Romania became *terra non gratia* in 1917 when they finally surrendered. The official line coming from the British war office was that Romania had done very little, and that they had been more a 'liability.' I can tell you however dear reader that German divisions were pulled out of where your boys were fighting to come down and knock out the Romanians, and at one place the Romanians scored a victory more heroic and convincing than anything your boys did in France. Needless to say I was known to the British mission there lead by Lieutenant-Colonel Christopher Thomson as a man who could be trusted, a patriot, maybe I was back then as well. Donald was the kind of man who never gets into history books, even if the Romanian campaign was in them. He seemed to have no rank, he didn't seem to even be a soldier, but he spoke Romanian, and he spoke it clearly and without any trace of an accent. In the time I knew him I heard him also speak German, Hungarian, Russian, Bulgarian and Serbian, although I can't say how fluent he was, but the last four languages he had only started learning since coming to Bucharest. It was Donald who had contacted me in 1926, he had gotten me out of that warehouse, he had told me that the job I had done in 1914 he wanted me to do again, and since it had been a wasted near decade since the end of the war I jumped at it. Of course Donald thought that I was the same man that I had been in 1917 when I had gotten him out through a country that was falling apart.

I watched the train pull into Worcester's Foregate Street station, bellowing out smoke down onto the street below, which was taken by the wind into the heart of the old city, like the ghost of the lost Viking. I knew that Donald was on that train, I knew he wouldn't be late, in the three and half years I had been with him on the forgotten front he had never been late. I got out of the car and headed up the steep steps which the smoke cascaded down like the mist in Dracula's castle. The passengers bound for Hereford drew forwards as the train stopped and were about to embark when the carriage door opened and a freakishly tall man bent double to get out. I smiled yes that was him, a little greyer maybe but that was him. He looked over the passengers as if they were exhibits in a zoo, "is this Foregate Street?" He asked with feint disdain.

"Yes sir," one of the passengers replied bowing slightly.

Donald nodded, "good." The passengers were about to get onto the train when the tall men extended his mahogany walking stick, "wait!" He snapped.

I chuckled. Then from the train a woman emerged holding a baby next to her ample bosom. She was nothing like the dark haired, Wallachian beauties I had sampled in the early years of the war but still she was the best I could hope for in England. Then I knew nothing about her, she might be Donald's wife, and the idea of fighting with him struck me like fighting with a giant mantis. The young woman weaved through the crowd of Herefordians and Donald looked across them sternly, before he slowly lowered his cane, "now! Now you can go on your way."

The train had come from London, the man had come from London but no one else knew anything about them here. I had parked the car in front of the Star Hotel, in front of a sign saying not to park there, but I knew no one would argue, not with this car, besides it made the hotel look more stylish than it was, with that car in front of it you half expected Douglas Fairbanks to sweep out through the revolving doors at any minute. I edged over and bowed slightly, making the height differential even worse. "Good to see you again Sir."

I hated myself for playing the humble London lackey again and Donald looked at me with the same coldness, "ah Simmonds good you are here, and the car?"

I then began to speak in Romanian, Donald's smile was more of a wince, but he replied to me. My eyes then fell on the young lady and she gave me the kind of smile that told me that I had a good chance with her. "I'm sorry to speak in a foreign tongue my lady, but it has been so long since I have used it, wanted to brush the rust away a little."

Donald looked at me coldly and reverted to English and I realized that I had my made my first *faux pas*, maybe Donald had not told her about his time in Romania, maybe he didn't want her to know, maybe it was still all secret. "See to the porter will you Simmonds, make sure he gets our baggage to the right place will you?"

As we headed down the steps I heard someone bellow out: "Bloody foreigners."

So there it was the great reunion, but then Romania had never been the same adventure to him that it had been to me, to my knowledge he had had no girlfriend there, no sweetheart, no whore , no romantic liaison, no woman he admired from afar. Neither had he been there at Marasesti, I'm not saying he was a coward but great, heroic battles were not his thing, he had killed, but coldly, not through passion. Still he had missed something that day when an army which belonged more in South America held the might of the Kaiser's hordes and saved Moscow, or so Romanian history books will tell you anyway.

Donald emerged into Foregate Street and looked down it towards the city like a slave master eyeing a new purchase, "Virgornia,' he murmured.

'Virgornia Sir?" The woman echoed.

"Yes that is it's Latin name, no doubt false middle ages Latin," Donald replied, "in the days when they were trying to make believe some great Roman past for this country."

My eyes fell on the woman, of course she didn't know what to say, no one spoke like that who she knew. I opened up the boot and let the porter put the baggage inside, of course it was up to me to give him a tip, that hadn't changed either. I seldom actually heard Donald ever use the word Worcester, he referred to the city either as Virgornia or Caerwrangon, which is the Welsh name, that was obviously some silly rule to what was going on here, some custom as stupid as Morris dancing. I watched the woman, who I later found out was called Matilda, when I had introduced myself, she nodded as he talked, and I could see that she was clever enough not to ask too many questions, that was good. "To most people this is just another city, but it is more than that."

"Yes," Matilda agreed but when she looked out of the window she just saw the same kind of streets that she had known in her own hometown. There were street urchins selling papers, hag faced women gossiping, men who were poor ex-grammar school boys who tried to make it look as if they had made it in life, but the threads hanging from their jackets betrayed them. It could have been Rochester, Chester, Chichester or a dozen other places. The whole country had changed though in the last twelve years, it was more a shadow land now, still reliving the nightmare of the war, only the people who were being born now were free of it, especially since no one liked talking about it. Before the war we had believed that we were invincible and that our leaders were wise, but the Germans had proved that we were all too beatable and both our parliament and our king had plunged us into hell. I thought about my son, God only knew what future he would have, I thought about my wife as well, she was beautiful whereas Matilda was only pretty, but as my father always said: 'All that glitters is not gold.'

Matilda held the baby close to her, but as the child yawned I caught sight of it's face, and I tried to pick out something of her in it, certainly I couldn't see Donald's bitter crow like features there. He bore the air of a stern butler that one of those huge country houses have, the kind of butler who has a dozen or so underlings to bully. I had the feeling that this wasn't his child and that he had just been called in as a clean up man, because you could see this was a child from a very rich and very powerful family.

Donald then remembered that I was a human being, "I am glad you made it Simmonds, I heard that you ended up on the Western Front."

I nodded, surprised that he had bothered to see what had become of me, maybe it was only because of this mission, certainly if he had known in 1918 he had done nothing to save me, "what about you Sir, what happened to you in the last year?"

"I stayed in Russia," Donald replied, "I stayed in Russia until the very end, I stayed longer than Kerensky, I stayed through the war and the civil war, that was a hell Simmonds, a real hell. Of course the Germans outplayed us there, they sent their man in, a German agent and he became president, you have to admire it in a way." His eyes then became distant, "they managed to awake a great devil from the Russian soul, a great evil, it is frightening what people will do to their own neighbours, their own family, even their own priests. I shudder to think what would have happened here if the Germans managed to summon up our demons."

"So all we did out there was for nothing?" I replied.

Donald smiled slightly, as if he had tried to have a conversation of one level only for it to revert to a lower one and he switched to Romanian confirming that what he was about to say was still classified, "no it was important without Romania we would have lost. People here don't realize how close we came to losing. They came in at a crucial time, we used them to get through it and after the war they got it all, every province, every village they had wanted. The Romanians are a people who live in the time of the Dacians, and they don't seem to realize that the great Roman province has seen wave of immigrations since: Szekler, Hungarian and Slav and whole areas now are filled with these people. They got it though, they got the Dacia of the Romans, with all it's Magyars, Slavs, Jews and Gypsies as well, but they won't hold it for long."

We drove down the high street, past the shop which still bore the name Elgar, because the composer's family still owned it. Matilda's eyes marveled at the cathedral and her thoughts had been the same as mine, wondering how men have ever built such a wonder, had they climbed all the way up there to carve the statues that were too high even for the iconoclasts to reach. "There is no building in London like that."

Donald nodded, "there was Saint Paul's."

"But," Matilda went to protest.

"I don't mean that half-Mohammedian nonsense, "Donald waved her away, "there was a proper cathedral once, like that one but the fire made it a ruin, and then the Stuarts destroyed the rest of it, and put their mosque there instead."

That little bit of conversation gave Matilda some courage and I noticed she edged off her seat a little, "what was that language you were speaking in?"

"English," Donald replied coldly, "sorry you didn't recognize it."

"No, the other language."

"Romanian," Donald replied.

"Are you Romanian?" She ventured.

"No."

"But you speak it," she tried again.

"Yes."

"But you are English?"

Donald sighed and nodded, "yes I am."

"But you speak Romanian?" Matilda added.

Donald nodded and sighed more deeply this time, like a school master facing an especially dim pupil, "I am an English man who can speak Romanian."

"And the driver," Matilda paused, "is he Romanian?"

"No," Donald moaned.

"But he can speak Romanian as well," Matilda protested.

"He is English as well."

"But-"

"He is an Englishman who can speak Romanian, like me."

"I've never met anyone who could speak Romanian," Matilda replied.

"Now you have met two," Donald smarted, still not introducing me. I then noticed Donald's eyes cross her face, her freckled nose, her lips, before settling sordidly on her large breasts. Of course she was a beneath the stairs type of person and normally he would never entertain ideas of courting such a low born wench, but I could see in his eyes he was running it through his mind, as if it was something he might have to do someday, some tedious chore.

"Where are we going Sir?" She tried again.

He drew towards her, "please call me Donald."

Matilda met his eyes, but any human warmth seemed false coming from him, "where are we going?" She asked again, not wanting to use his name.

The tall man drew back, "once the family had four castles here, there was one here in the city itself, one on the slopes of Bredon Hill at Emley and one on the other side of the river at Hanley, but they were lost during the war."

"The Great War Sir?"

Donald smiled, "no the Kaiser's baboons never got this far, the civil war Matilda, the civil war, when all the scum of Scotland and England rose up against their King. This land was the most faithful part of his realm, that's why it suffered the most during the republic. Emley is now just ditches and a few rocks in a wood where no one ever visits."

"So where are we going?" She tried again.

"The only castle left," Donald replied, "Holt."

We crossed the river Severn over a bridge of balustrades, "this is the first river of the country Matilda, not the one in London, it rises in the mountains of Wales, in the lair of Owen Glendower. The Thames rises in some muddy field near Cirencester," Donald smiled, "hardly inspiring is it?"

I drew back and smiled, I was back in Bucharest in 1914, Donald had been like that then, it had been the only time that I had ever seen him animated, he was no leader really, and he could not enthuse his men or anyone, but sometimes passion crept into his cold frame.

We turned right past the gate of cripples where the poorest and most afflicted people of the city begged to save themselves from starvation. Hardly did they look like people belonging to a race who had conquered the world, they were the ghosts of war, leaning on crutches, disfigured, blinded. I looked at them, I could have been there, imagine losing your eyes just so we British could keep the Germans out of our protected markets, if that's what it had been all about. All of them should have been living in big houses in Germany with an army of Teutonic slaves to serve them, but they had gotten nothing in exchange for the legs and their eyes and their futures. Donald glanced at them, I didn't know what he thought when he saw such people, maybe he viewed them as just the biological wastage of war. Certainly the Kaiser was living better than they were in retirement in Holland, Lloyd George had harangued about getting him hung, but he had won the election and nothing had happened, wasn't the first time that had happened.

Donald had given me instructions to take the Tenbury Road out of Worcester and we went along the river before climbing up a bank and slowing at a fork, two signs stood before me and they both said the same thing: 'Tenbury Wells.' "What is the meaning of this?"

"Yes, they both say the same thing," Matilda gasped.

There was something weird about that sign, as if it made sense to someone somewhere, that someone had to be Donald, "yes because they both go to the same place, just as there is more than one way to skin a cat then there is more than one way to go from Worcester to Tenbury Wells."

I nodded and just looked at the sign; both arrows were exactly the same, "I have never even heard of Tenbury Wells, it doesn't seem important enough to have one road let alone two."

Donald pointed to the left arrow, "that goes over a great hill."

I pointed to the other fork, "then that way is flat?"

"No it goes over a hell of a hill at Abberley," Donald smiled.

"Then what is the point of it?" I asked.

"Take the right fork Simmonds, that is where we want to go," Donald then sank back and nodded, like a college kid who had just come up against an exam question that he had revised for. It had always been hard to understand Donald's motivation, he hardly seemed a great patriot or royalist, more a realist, and he saw people for what they were. In Romania it had certainly all brushed past him, he never got enveloped in all the hate that blew and I should imagine still blows over that land, he treated everyone the same Gypsy, Jew and German. He never insulted my intelligence either by using words like Hun and Bosh, he never trotted out that retelling of history that others did. He passed Germans in the streets in those days, of course, and he just looked the other way, they were not his enemies they were more like his opponents as if it was a game of chess. The day Romania had crossed the mountains they had met him in the street and started to spit hate, Donald had only smiled weakly and wished them better luck next time and that the game had moved onto Washington. All of us in those days expected the Yanks to go in on the German side because they had always hated us and because they wanted us out of Ireland, someone must have done a wonder job over there to get them to come in on our side.

The last vestiges of the city faded and we entered the apple orchards the county was famous for, rolling like carpets of white blossom down from the hillsides stopping only at the rivers to outstretch their branches to their branches of their brothers on the opposite bank. This was the England we had been fighting for I guess, God knows what would have happened if the Kaiser had won, I doubt he would have pulled up all the apple orchards, and our King was a German anyway. A great church spire rose up above the trees, "Hallow." Donald whispered.

"Sorry?" Matilda frowned.

Donald smiled, "it is the name of the village my dear, I have only seen it in black and white before, and then in two dimensions."

Of course I wanted to ask him what this was all about, in London I had thought that this was a normal job that maybe it was a payback for what I had done in the war, but a lot of people had done things during the war and never got anything for it. With every minute it was becoming clearer and clearer that this was not going to be a normal job. Still the Worcestershire countryside seemed innocent enough not like the dark mountain passes of the war and the vast bleak plain of the east, there was something unnerving about a country with an endless horizon, even a treeless tundra could hide a hundred Germans. I looked in the rear view mirror and met his darker than brown eyes, I was about to look away when he spoke in Romanian again:

"There is one thing that troubles me about you Simmonds."

"What is that Sir?" I replied.

"Your time in Romania," Donald began, "people say that you went native there."

"What do you mean?" I frowned.

"Marasesti," Donald replied, "it wasn't your fight, what was it to you if the Romanians got wiped out there or not?"

"I saw there were Germans to kill there and I killed them, we were at war with them," I replied.

"People said that you weren't fighting for Merry Olde England but the Kingdom of Romania, there was a story that you risked your life to save a dozen of them who had gotten themselves cut off, that you rescued them, killing several Germans to do it."

"An exaggeration I think, you know what people are like," I replied.

"Oh come, come Simmonds you are being modest, Thomson got a report from a certain Lieutenant Sima, he greatly praised your courage, he said you were one of them," Donald paused and then repeated,, "one of them. No one could tell the difference between you an Englishman and them a pack of white Latin savages! You shouldn't have done it," Donald chided.

"They were our allies," I retorted, forgetting to add 'Sir.'

"The French were our allies, the Americans were our allies, the Romanians were," Donald paused searching for the right word and then could not find it, "not. I'm sure Sima thought that he was doing you a favour, but he was not, that is what got you posted to the trenches. Thomson hoped that you would die there and your secrets with you."

I could only reply to that with silence.

"Stop at this crossroads," Donald coughed. So I slowed the car at a crossroads and read the arrows. Tenbury Wells carried out to the west climbing like a crazed cyclist up a bank towards some foreboding, wooded hills, where the ancients had built their citadel against the Romans. There was something Carpathian about that way, a darkness about it, only whatever savagery had gone on there had been centuries ago. At least in England you could go anywhere, in Transylvania you'd have to find out who lived there first, Vlach, Szekler, Hungarian or whatever, the road in front of us said 'Stourport.'

Donald pointed there, "that's where Stanley Baldwin lives, British Prime Minister and bastard," he then remembered Matilda was there, "sorry."

The right arrow said 'Droitwich.' Donald nodded towards it, "Droitwich it is Simmonds."

I turned the car right down a bank which seemed to plummet down towards the Severn, I could see it glistening through the branches.

Chapter Two: Welcome to Holt Castle.

Reading back on what I have written so far I notice I have mentioned Al Jolson and Douglas Fairbanks twice, I guess three times now. You can let me off Fairbanks, the first time I was talking about the son, the second time the father. I don't know why I bother, I doubt this is ever going to get published, I doubt it will ever even get out of this house, they will find it, maybe I should make a copy, but then who cares? I don't even know why I care anymore. The thing about West Beverley is this: I am in the heart of the world, it is all swirling around me, it is only a short bus ride to Paramount Studios, I could make it to Santa Monica beach in an hour, if I ran. Yet it is as if I am on the far side of the earth. All the little things that make up another city are gone from this place; it is almost like one of their film sets that look convincing until you look closely, the great stones which make up the castle look too neat, too precise, not hammered out of some Saxon quarry somewhere. The ivy climbing it's walls look like it's been taken out of a landscape garden, not some unwanted pest that just sprouted up and had been hacked at several times but kept growing back. No set maker would ever have made Holt Castle, things look different in West Beverley, but I can still smell the aromas of the English countryside, as sweetly as if it was yesterday, and I can still remember my first sight of the castle:

I took the limousine down that road and thought that I was heading down towards the river before Donald's crow like nose edged into my sight, "up there!"

I looked up what looked like nothing more than a gap in a hedge, "up there Sir?"

Donald slowly nodded, "yes up there Simmonds, what's the matter do you want me to say it in Romanian?"

I sighed knowing that I would spend hours cleaning this car afterwards, waxing and polishing it, still I eased on the accelerator and we headed up the narrow track of rocks and mud. Donald's fingernails dug into the car's armrest and he cursed through gritted teeth and the car rocked from side to side like a rowing boat heading down the Danube. Matilda uttered several prayers and looked heavenwards, once even I thought that we were heading straight into a ditch only for the road to curve round and my eyes met two great towers as old as the Normans. Both had that centuries worn look about them, they were like two old men staring down at me, the kind of old men who had seen us go to war in 1914 and had only shaken their heads. One was the church the other was the castle, there was nothing else here in the ancient village of Holt, a great hedge surrounded it on three sides and, the land plummeted down to the river on the other. My eyes ran along that hedge, never had I seen one like it, it must have been twice my height at least; this hedge was what closed it off from the rest of the world. "You won't find this place on any maps," Donald noted.

"Why?" Matilda gasped.

"How?"I asked, almost at the same time.

Donald chuckled, "we have wiped it off the maps, all the maps."

"But why?" Matilda repeated.

Donald tensed and ignored her.

This place would have fascinated any rambler or amateur historian, but they never got here. This never appeared on any ordinance survey maps, we were less than two hour's drive from London and yet this was more remote, more mysterious than those Carpathian ruins I use to explore back in those early, halcyon days of the war. Looking back on it here from West Beverley it does seem hard to see how they kept it a secret for so long, but then the castle could be seen from neither road nor river.

The hedge relented for a small fence, the kind you would see outside of a thousand farms across the land, on it hung a sign, which was written in Latin, French and then reluctantly English: 'Keep ye out, private!' Matilda's eyes ran along it then suddenly darted back as a face appeared before vanishing again, she gasped.

"What is it?"I asked.

"I saw something," she replied.

"What?" I asked.

"It looked like a dog," she replied.

"That's no dog," I replied as I saw it as well, it looked straight at me and yawned, a man's head could disappear into that mouth.

"It is a Tasman wolf, we had them brought over here from Van Diemen's land," Donald explained.

"Wolves?!" Matilda gasped.

We both laughed, how could it be that an English girl feared wolves as much as a Transylvanian peasant? They had gone from this land for centuries, yet the folk memory was still there, maybe thanks to Red Riding Hood or maybe a deeper fear that was engrained in her heart. This had once been their land, before any of the human conquerors had even been dreamt of, man had defeated the wolf, had driven him off his land but had never enslaved him: A wolf cannot be tamed, cannot not be made to jump through hoops like a lion, a wolf would rather go to hell than serve man, rather bite his arm off that accept his charity.

"It was no wolf either," I muttered. I had looked into a wolf's eyes before and it was as like looking into the eyes of an old rival, these eyes had little memory of mankind. Gently I applied the breaks before the fence, because that was where the road ended and I turned to Donald, "now what?"

Donald just looked at me and sighed before getting out as he did a craggy faced man appeared behind the fence, "can't ye read? It says piss off!"

Like a good soldier my eyes fell to the shot gun his hands tightened around, "he's got a gun Sir!"

Donald smiled and looked back at me, "first time you ever saw one Simmonds? What did the Germans have at Marasesti then? Peashooters?" His eyes then turned to the stranger, "I can of course read Mr Fitzroy."

"How do you know my name? If you are from the tax again I told you to phone that number in London, if you don't phone them and come here again you'll disappear, you don't know what land you are stepping onto, there is the outside world and then there is here. Now for your own good get back in your motorcar and head back to wherever you came from, whether it be London, Burning Ham or your old lady's fanny!"

Donald chuckled at that, "I have come from the first of those places but I cannot go back." Fitzroy was about to argue when Donald held up his hand to silence him. "I cannot go back because I am the new bearer of the secret."

Fitzroy stepped back and his gun sank a little, "what secret?"

"A child has been born!" Donald announced.

Fitzroy nodded, he resembled a little an old fox cornered by a wolf, "I yeard a child had been born, but.."

Donald smiled, "and so there was and I have the other child," his eyes flitted back to the car.

Fitzroy hesitated as if somehow his whole world had stopped, and we froze with him, then suddenly he snapped back to life and beat back the animals before opening the gate which gave out a great rasping moan as if it too was a prisoner here. Then our eyes crossed the beasts which looked midway between dog and rat, as big as any wolf with their hind quarters striped like a tiger's. Somehow I was relieved to see that they were not wolves and yet there was another fear, the fear of the unknown."Have you ever seen such a thing?" Matilda asked.

I shook my head, "no never."

Donald got back inside the car and smiled in contentment, "drive on."

"I'm sorry?"

"Drive on," he repeated.

"Into that zoo?" I gasped.

"What are you afraid Simmonds?" He gasped, "I remember you back in Romania, I saw you with my own eyes I don't need no Romanian officer to tell me, I saw you face death myself and you weren't afraid then."

"Maybe I'm getting old," I replied.

Donald smiled, "those animals are quite tame Simmonds, quite tame."

"Good then you get out first," I replied before adding, "Sir."

Fitzroy beckoned us to enter before sinking to his knee as the car came to a halt, "Lord I am thy servant."

Donald slowly got out of the car and his hand rested on Fitzroy's head, "so it was and so it will be

again. "

I looked back at Matilda, to her eyes it reminded her of a pantomime, "what the hell have we gotten ourselves into?"

Fitzroy hurried over to the gate and dragged it close, the beasts just watched him, not one of them had made a break for freedom, and their dark eyes just looked at the space as if their world ended there. Donald's eyes met Fitzroy's as he headed back, "you know if one of them got out it would be big news."

"Why is that?" I asked.

Donald never replied to me, my eyes were fixed on the way they moved; it seemed strangely un-dog like. Then I looked at the castle, only the great square tower survived from the original building, the rest of the house was only two hundred years in age, hardly like the great castles along the Welsh border, those looked like the lairs of giants. Holt fell more into the fortified manor house ranks meant to repel more a wandering band of Welshmen, certainly it would have been swept away by the full massed ranks of Glendower's finest.

"You know my Lord," Fitzroy added, "this is an ancient land; people have lived here since before two thousand years before the birth of our Lord and Saviour."

"He means Jesus," I whispered back to Matilda.

"The Romans passed this place over," Fitzroy continued, "they left all it's ancientness in tact, they only butchered the people here and left an edict that no man more should live here. Of course the Saxons knew nothing of that, they didn't even know how to read, so they settled here and gave it it's name Holt, meaning little wood, after the wood that the Romans had let grow over the bones of the old ones."

Matilda looked at the castle as if it was a great palace but to Donald it was a measly little place he nodded, "thank you Fitzroy, I still have much to learn."

"Why did the Romans want nobody living here?" I asked.

Fitzroy grinned a grin of crooked yellow, he had wanted that question, "because they said the old ones were evil, witches and that kind, that's why they killed them and they said no one should live here because they had soiled the earth with their darkness."

Donald nodded, of course there was no way Fitzroy could have known what the Romans had thought, he had probably made it up himself, or one of his imbecilic predecessors had. He then looked back at me, and handed me a piece of paper, "these are the directions to Dunstall Common."

I just looked at the paper, "where?"

"Go there, there you will find a tower, which was built some years ago for our purpose. There you will live with your woman if you have one, and children if you have any. There is a telephone connected, we will phone you at seven every evening to give you your instructions for the next day."

I frowned, "you mean I am not staying here with you?"

"You can see there is no room here," he replied.

"I stayed in worse places in Romania," I retorted.

"Huh," he snorted, "but you are not in Romania now, you are amidst civilized people."

I looked at Fitzroy and shook my head.

"Now go Simmonds, you have three days before we contact you again, that should be long enough for you to settle into your new home," he then looked down the side of the car. "And for God's sake clean this car up."

I nodded, of course I should asked more questions but I remembered then that this was a job, that I was getting paid, indeed I had already been paid, my wife was already spending the money. "Thank you Sir." I looked at the strange dogs and their even stranger master and I was glad not to be staying here, then my eyes met Matilda's. She was the only reasons that I wanted to stay, she saw me as the only sane one here, now I was leaving her to the madhouse. A woman hurried out from the castle she looked like Fitzroy and I thought she was his sister before he introduced her to Donald as his wife. She was the one who dragged the gate open, as I drove through I looked back at Matilda, God help her.

I didn't know much more after that, I followed Donald's directions south along the river. I could understand how people could worship rivers whether it be the Ganges in India or Osun in Nigeria, where the natives believe she was once the wife of god who had been turned into a river. The Severn is such a river, there was more than just water in it, it was as if the thing was alive itself, like a huge snake slowly moving south through the land. There is a river here, where I am now, but it runs in a vast drainage ditch like the one in Birmingham does, a city loses it's soul when it does that to it's river because a river is as much a part of a city as it's people or it's great temple.

I headed south so I have to rely on Matilda's memory as to what happened after I had left her there: Donald's eyes settled on Fitzroy's wife, certainly he didn't envy him that task. He bowed slightly towards her: "You have no children my lady?"

Her face crumpled slightly, as if he had just kicked open a grave and Fitzroy hurried forwards, "yes we have my Lord but they have long since gone."

"What they never visit?" Donald asked.

Fitzroy's face then creased, "they can't from heaven my Lord. They both died in the war."

"Oh I'm sorry," it was as if it was only now he had found his senses and was human again, his eyes then fell on a simple man. A family quarrel inside the royal family that ruled Europe had dragged in the French and American republics, the Japanese, the Thais, Chinese had come to work in the trenches, all sacrifices to the great god Mars, who that family worship behind their pretence of Christianity. Millions had been slaughtered and yet these humble peasants had never blamed their masters, only in Russia had they figured it out.

"They will be waiting for me there though," Fitzroy added.

Donald nodded. God knew if any of that was true or fairy tales. I had seen Donald in churches in Romania, in the dark painted caves of Orthodoxy where he had stood as if outside of everything, never crossing himself never joining in with the chants. I had thought that it was just that he wasn't Orthodox, but then I had seen him in the English church in the middle of Bucharest and he had been the same there, like a shadow in the place, a ghost from somewhere else, he had been there but his eyes were far far away. Even if there was a God none of it would make up for Fitzroy losing his sons.

"My brother died in the war," Donald replied after a dignified pause, "leading an assault on the cliffs at Gallipoli."

Fitzroy looked at him and nodded, but one brother didn't equal two sons and they both knew it, "yes nasty business that was Sir, bloody Germans."

Donald nodded, he thought that it was better not to mention the uncle he had had who died fighting for the Germans or that in fact it had been the bloody Turks at Gallipoli.

Inside the castle it was more modern than Matilda would have thought, there was a coat of armour but Fitzroy had bought it a few years back from a place in Droitwich, thinking no castle was complete without one, when you looked at it you could see that it was not genuine. There were no paintings of the previous lords just pictures of random places. As Matilda walked in holding the baby both Fitzroys tried to get a look at her, "is it a girl?" The woman asked.

"Well of course it is a girl," Donald sighed, "if it had been a boy the other one would be here, but unfortunately they are both girls."

Fitzroy nodded and shook his head, "I hope our Mr Hannover hasn't got himself some useless wench who can only give us girls."

Matilda could only frown at their conversation, she knew the baby wasn't Donald's, but who was Mr Hanover?

Donald smiled and played with his cuff a little, he wasn't use to Fitzroy's lack of reverence.

Fitzroy's eyes fell on the baby's face with some pity; she had lost the lottery of life, where there had only been two numbers, "is this the *kehinde* then?"

Donald smiled, another test, Fitzroy still didn't trust him completely, and only someone inside the secret or who spoke Yoruba would know that word, "yes of course the *taiwo* is with the mother."

Fitzroy backed away and nodded. In the past someone had brought those words back from Africa because the English language never had words that meant the same. He looked down at the baby again, so this was the mirror image, so the Romans believed. He had begun to think over the years that it was better to bring both babies here because a twin is only half a person, and how could a Halfling be left with such power? Donald had passed the test anyway and he nodded, "very good my Lord."

"Do you go into VIrgornia much Fitzroy?" Donald then asked.

Fitzroy then nodded, reassured again at his use of that word, "sometimes when the house needs something for it's repair, or to buy the necessities of life, but then I normally stay in the Welsh town, seldom do I cross the river into all those crowds and confusion."

Donald almost laughed out loud; he made Worcester sound like New York.

"But better still I goes to Droitwich, if I can get me a ride there," Fitzroy added as he struggled with their luggage up the stairs. "Otherwise I walk."

Fitzroy carried Matilda's luggage into a room where there was a crib, it had not been used in a century, certainly their own sons had never lain there but they had kept it in immaculate condition. In fact the whole house was like a museum. Donald entered the room like a tour guide, "this is where you will sleep with the baby Matilda."

Matilda walked over to the window and looked down on the river, she shares my draw to them, it is why part of her is withering here now in West Beverley. There is something so soulful about looking into the depths of a great river, Neanderthals had looked upon that river, as had the Welsh and the Romans, all had gone but the river was still there. The bridge the English had built over it would one day fall into it and be swept away, but the river would continue, but then rivers could die in droughts and that was as painful to watch as to see any animal die. Matilda looked at the bridge which they would have crossed if they gone onto Droitwich, she had only just got here but she already felt like a prisoners as she watched the people walk over it.

They felt it was best to let Matilda settle in and so headed to Donald's room, Fitzroy then drew close to him, "who is that girl my Lord?"

"She is someone the family knew of."

"Do you trust her?" Fitzroy snapped, forgetting to put 'sir.'

Donald stopped and turned on him, as he had done many times to some Romanian official who was beginning to get ideas above his station. His glare reminded Fitzroy that he was nothing, just a creature scurrying around an old castle with an ugly wife, "I trust no one Fitzroy."

Fitzroy though wasn't intimidated, he was stood on the ground his family had lived on for centuries, "we don't need her, and my wife can look after the nipper."

Donald leant forwards, "we need her dear Fitzroy because of her breasts, they are expressing milk, I take it your wife's are not."

Fitzroy still was undaunted, "then if they are expressing milk," he paused having just mastered the word, "where is the baby the milk was for?"

"Dead," Donald replied, "it was a late miscarriage."

He thought that was to settle it but Fitzroy rounded again like a bull terrier, "and the father then? I bet she never had one."

Donald laughed, "I'm sure you realize Fitzroy that that is impossible."

"The husband I meant, I bet she never had one! I bet she is one of those cheap whores who wander round London like a bloody tribe! There are so many down there!"

Donald drew back like a stern Presbyterian minister, "that is enough Fitzroy, you must never speak ill of Matilda again, do you hear me?"

Fitzroy nodded grudgingly, "yes my Lord."

"You have done well so far, you have kept the house well, do not spoil it now."

Fitzroy nodded, "yes my Lord."

Donald paused though; there was something that troubled him, why did he say Mr Hannover? Where did that come from? "Do you get any trouble from the locals Fitzroy?"

Fitzroy chuckled with contempt, "what them? There are two villages, that ramshackle you might have passed at the crossroads is called Holt Heath. The one down by the river is called Holt Fleet, that place gets flooded every year or so, every year they get washed out of their houses, I watch from here and see their belongings go floating by to be fished out downstream somewhere. Every year they say never again but every March they go back to them, they don't have the brains to move up to the Heath. But them the folk down at the Fleet are different from the ones on the Heath. The ones on the Heath are the old people who always lived here, the ones on the Fleet are trash who had gotten off boats coming down from Shrewsborough or up from Glevum, they have gotten off the boats and for some reason never got on again, which is their illustrious parentage. The children are full of stories about this place, they say it's haunted, but you know when you are that age every where is haunted even your wardrobe, but the dogs keep them at bay."

Donald smiled weakly, "please lead the way." Fitzroy then lead him into a room which was larger and grander with a four poster bed. The tall man nodded, yes this would do, it's windows faced the other way looking out over West Worcestershire to where Abberley clock tower rose like a great Egyptian needle towards the sky, there the road to Tenbury Wells disappeared. On the hill next to it (Woodbury) the Duke of Buckingham had arrived centuries ago with an army of Welshmen keen to turf Richard III off the throne, but as soon as they had reached there they had seen all their dreams perish. From there they had looked down over to a river Severn that had flooded, the floods stopped them from joining their allies deeper into England, it was like a small sea stretching out before them, a wall of water it needed sailors not soldiers to cross. Buckingham's army deserted him as if he had the plague; he was captured and killed at Salisbury. That river had saved the king and sentenced his enemy to hell.

Fitzroy followed his master's eyes, "there are many places to walk to over there, and only the ghosts will bother you, no one else will, you can walk as far as Salopshire if you like."

Donald smiled to himself, Shrewsborough, Salopshire, Burning Ham, only Droitwich it seemed was honoured enough to be called by it's proper name, and London, but then he had many other names for that place as well. "Maybe I will do so in the summer. You know well the traditions of the Lord of Holt Castle," Donald conceded.

"So I should do," Fitzroy conceded, "it has been my life, as it was my father's life, we wait here like the Jews wait for their Messiah to come, we wait for a new Lord, for a new child to be born, a child whose fate has been caused to be born twice. This has been the life of my family back to the time of Good King John, but I guess the Huns have ended that now."

Donald nodded, "yes, I am sorry, they destroyed many things, many lives, even their own in the end."

"Yes they have a strange blood that is for sure," Fitzroy nodded. "The thing I don't get is this: If we have such a great empire, that spans the globe, that includes Maoris, and Muslims and Hindus and Sikhs, and we've got Maltese and Zulus, and Aborigines as black as the night and.."

"Yes so what?" Donald cut in.

Fitzroy's eye rested on him, "then why didn't they send them off to fight the Hun? Folk people don't give a rat's ass about, you could lose millions of them and no one would notice, why do they send people from places like this out to get killed? I mean what's the point in having all these people in our empire if we ain't going to use them!"

Donald then leant forwards like a kindly old uncle, "the trouble is Fitzroy is if we give those people Enfield rifles they would turn them on us. After all if is us who they are trying to free themselves from, not the Germans, many of them even see the Germans as their liberators, they pray for the Germans to arrive where they are, they forget about what they did in Namibia."

Fitzroy thought about what he had said and then nodded, "maybe you are right Sir. Are you hungry my Lord? My wife is an excellent cook."

She would have to be with that face because he never married her for her looks, Donald thought, "what is on the menu?"

"Pheasant and cider," Fitzroy declared.

"Pheasant and cider," Donald mused, "well there are certainly worse ways to spend the rest of my life."

"Oh there is wine down in the cellar, I do not go down there much but-"

Donald interrupted him, "no cider will be fine, will wash away all that wine you drink down in the capital and after all I am in the county of Virgornia now, best go native."

Fitzroy nodded, not knowing if he was being mocked or not, "I'd best take my leave of you then Sir."

"Yes thank you Fitzroy," Donald then replied before adding under his breath, "Mr Hanover."

Fitzroy was still bowing as he closed the door until it shut before his back straightened and headed down stairs with a purpose, he went straight to the one bag he hadn't brought upstairs and was going to go through it when he saw his wife already attacking it like a seagull, "what the hell are you doing?"

"Looking at his books," she snapped.

"Didn't know you could read," he mocked.

"I read well enough to know what that says," she replied and came out of his briefcase brandishing a prize, "look what it says 'Das Kapital' by Karl Marx!"

Fitzroy waggled his finger at her, "that's one of them Marxist books that is!"

Mrs Fitzroy nodded, "it's Marx himself!"

Fitzroy drew back and ran his fingers through his hair, "then he's one of them! He's a Bolshevik, Marxist, Leftist sod!"

His wife smiled and shrugged, "maybe he just likes to read."

"And which library does he go to the one in Petrograd?! What are the others?"

"Dickens, Keats, Shakespeare, HG Wells," she replied looking through them.

"HG Wells!" Fitzroy seized on that one alright, "he's one of them leftist, disloyal communist bastard, what's the book about?"

"The Invisible Man," she replied.

"Probably a book about Lenin," Fitzroy snorted.

Lightly she eased the book back into the briefcase before drawing the latch back, "we are going to have to watch our guest very carefully."

"And that woman he's brought with him," Fitzroy added, "we need to watch her as well, you wouldn't believe where he found her!"

"Where?"

"A house of prostitutes! "

Mrs Fitzroy gasped and drew back with her hand over her mouth, "oh my Lord! Yes I think we have stumbled into something here, my love."

Fitzroy nodded, "yes you're not wrong there love, you're not wrong there."

Chapter Three: Dinner with the Fitzroys.

The last thing Matilda wanted after the miscarriage was to be near to another baby, but she needed the work. Times were hard, they had been hard during the war, but they had been kept going through the hunger by the lies pouring out through the papers that the world would be better after it had all finished. Their men would return as victors and conquerors, her father had returned alright, at least a man had arrived at the house who had looked like her father, but he had been distant and had spoken in one or two words only, and he had gone after a month and never returned. The Jazz Age never seemed to settle on England, things were still poor, and so when she met the man of her dreams, good looking and rich of course she gave him everything, she never did tell me his name but I can kind of guess who he was. The baby had been born too soon to live and had died in her arms, she had buried him in a corner of the cemetery where there were no stones, and she had cried it was as if her whole world had been torn in two. However her eyes had opened in the rain to see that she was still with the hunger, she had lost her job because of that pregnancy, her only choice was to beg the baby's father for help and he had gotten her this job. So the baby from nowhere was now drinking the milk meant for her own child. She sat there and gazed down into the river and imagined herself falling into it and flying through the water into another world. Her eyes fell onto the baby's pretty face and she tried to find something of Donald there, but there was nothing, if he wasn't her father then who was he? Maybe a man somewhere was longing to see his little daughter and what of her mother?

A knock came at the door, "please come in."

Matilda hurriedly covered her breast and the baby's head, as the door slowly opened and Fitzroy came in with a cup of tea. "There we are my dear."

"Thank you Mr Fitzroy."

He nodded, "the lady will not be wanting to go out will she?" It was as if he had to force himself to say 'lady' as if the word did not pass his lips willingly.

"No it is getting dark."

Fitzroy gave a smile of false kindness, "because I let the animals out in the courtyard after dark."

"They can't come in here can they?" She asked.

"No they have not yet mastered the door knob, or can they indeed unbolt the door," Fitzroy replied. "I will bring you up some food then my lady, some pheasant and a little drop of cider."

She laughed, "you are kind."

His face stung at the slight Cockney edge to her voice before he looked down at the infant, "giving the baby some milk are you?"

She blushed slightly, "yes."

He smiled with a false warmth as he watched the baby's mouth open and close silently, "looks like the little nipper wants some more."

Matilda looked away and pulled her coat up around her breasts, "maybe later."

"Yes of course," he smiled again and Matilda shuddered, he would never make an actor, unless it was one of those overblown ham actors who always get the plaudits and ended up with a knighthood. He drew back a bit before edging forwards again. "Do you know whose baby it is?"

"No," she replied.

Fitzroy's face warmed and he dangled the carrot in front of her eyes, and repeated more firmly this time, "do you know whose baby that is?"

"No," she replied again, "and I do not want to."

"Don't you care?"

Matilda's eyes then drilled into his, "my mother is a poor widow, I need this job."

Fitzroy nodded, "but doesn't it interest you at all whose little mouth is sucking on your tit?"

Matilda shook her head, "it is not my business who the baby's father and mother are, just as long as my mother keeps getting the money."

"What if I told you," Fitzroy leant forwards again and she got the smell of damp clothes and cow pats. "What if I told you that her last name is Romanov, that she in fact is the last of them?"

Matilda nodded, paused and then shrugged, "who?"

"The Kings of Russia," Fitzroy magically replied.

"Then what is she doing here?" Matilda retorted.

"Don't you know anything girl? Don't you read the papers? They were all murdered! All of them! If any of them escaped, anyone of them, then people would come after them!" Fitzroy declared.

"Who?"

"The people who murdered the rest of them of course!"

Matilda felt a chill run through her, "murderers?"

Fitzroy nodded, "yes."

Matilda clung to the baby tightly, and then looked away, "still it is not my business, talk to Donald about it, I'm sure he knows about security."

Fitzroy paused, "yes you're probably right my dear, you're probably right. We'd probably best leave it there for tonight." He bowed a little before heading towards the door before suddenly stopping as Donald came in: "Good evening Sir."

"Good evening Fitzroy," Donald smiled and watched the servant leave before he turned to Matilda, "I hope he wasn't bothering you."

"No he asked me if I wanted something to eat," she replied.

Donald looked back, as if he could see through the door before gazing back and whispering, "what do you think of them?"

"Well they are kind of creepy."

Donald nodded, "they have been too long alone here."

"How long have they been here?"

"Forever," Donald replied and looked around the room as if it was cursed, before adding, "it is rather cut off here."

"You make it sound like some Scottish island, this is the middle of England," Matilda protested.

"In some ways," Donald sneered.

"There is a village and a pub," she added.

Donald nodded, "there are but they seldom go there. The Fitzroys are an old, old family, who cannot mix with the rest of the people in this part of the county."

"Why?"

"This place must remain a secret! If they set foot inside the village pub they will be hit by a dozen questions, no they have to stay here, you understand don't you?"

Matilda looked up at him, "you don't expect me to say yes do you Sir?"

Donald smiled, "I can see you are a clever girl. You have entered something which goes back to the time of King John. They do not think you should have been brought into this because your blood is not part of it, but then neither is mine."

"Fitzroy mentioned the Romanovs," Matilda replied.

Donald frowned, "the Romanovs?"

"Yes, he just told me that the baby was theirs."

Donald nodded, "did he? Well I suppose she is a distant relative of theirs."

Matilda smiled, "you speak in riddles, I do not wish to know anything, I am here to do a job, not be part of something you might see in the music hall."

Donald smiled, "yes you might be right. Will you come down and partake in dinner?"

She looked down at the baby, she was asleep, "I had best put this little one in her bed first."

Donald hovered for a moment and then realized that Matilda would show her breast and apologized, "oh I am sorry, I will see you downstairs."

There was no great hall, the Lord of Holt Castle was a very minor noble, who had never even got a mention in Burke's Peerage. Still there was a long mahogany table which Donald could sit at the head of and imagine he was somewhere else, Windsor great hall or someplace like that. His eyes crossed Mrs Fitzroy's face as she served him with the pheasant, potatoes and vegetables before pouring gravy over it before he could ask for it or not. Donald noticed she had the same ears as her husband; exactly the same, now what were the chances of that?

"May we join you Sir?" Fitzroy asked, "because I am afraid that this is the only table in the house."

"Yes of course Fitzroy, please do."

Fitzroy sat down and his eyes glinted as the plate was laid down before him, "now that is what a dinner should look like."

"Yes quite so," Donald agreed.

"I was so afraid when my boys went to France," Fitzroy continued, "I mean them folk don't eat properly."

"French cuisine is renowned all over the world," Donald countered.

"That may be the case," Fitzroy replied, "but it ain't no bloody good."

Donald smiled again, "yes quite so, tell me –er Mr Fitzroy where do you get all the food from?"

Fitzroy smiled, "a lot of the stuff we can grow ourselves and we have some fowl, pigs and sheep in the land between here and the river, but if this is not enough for you I can cross the river and climb the hill to the butchers in Ombersley, it is only half an hour's walk. It is all up hill, but then it is down hill on the way back."

Donald smiled, "yes that would be nice in the future."

"Ombersley is a proper village," Fitzroy continued, "not that shanty town over there or that glorified slum down by the river. The people are proper people too, not the refuge and beggars we have around here, any good people moved from the Holt villages years ago, no centuries ago and now we are left with the human half beings, you know the kind *your* Mr Darwin says that we all came from."

There was nothing gentile or sophisticated about the way Fitzroy ate with his elbows boldly on the table and he seemed to shovel the food in as if he was in a hurry, but surely here he had nothing but time? At least he knew not to speak with his mouth full, Donald hated that, he had cursed the Slavs when he had seen them do it. Donald looked at him wondering if this is what King John would have looked like, that is who Fitzroy was meant to have descended from, but the blood must have been greatly diluted with some strange village stock since then, there was certainly nothing regal about him now.

Fitzroy's eyes suddenly shot up at him, "it was a nasty business in Russia wasn't it?"

Donald nodded slowly, "yes, but I fear it is all over now."

"As if we didn't have enough of war before, but they had to fight each other. It's not decent that folk should turn on their King and kill him and his family," Fitzroy continued.

Donald shrugged and seemed disinterested, "we did the same once at the time of Cromwell."

"They did," Fitzroy sneered and motioned to where the floorboards creaked beneath Matilda's feet.

"Who?"

"Londoners, it wasn't us here! The honest folk of this shire stayed loyal to our King: Charles Stuart. We lost our castles for it and the wall around the sacred city was brought down so that we couldn't resist anymore, that abomination of a republic! There are no republics in the bible! Republics are born from hell!" There was a fire in Fitzroy's eyes, a fanaticism; he spoke as if it had all happened last year.

"Charles Stuart," Donald mused.

Fitzroy continued, "it was that rabble in London who killed the king not us up here! I mean it ain't natural for a people not to have a king, heaven has a king there are kings in the bible that is for sure!" Then he stopped as if he had only just heard, "what did you say?"

Donald ignored him, "your family is an old one Fitzroy, never mind the Stuarts you are descended from the Plantagenets, and some would say that your blood is nobler than the people who occupy the throne today."

Fitzroy shook his head, "noble? How can I be noble when my ancestor was a bastard?"

Donald smiled delicately, "the story I read was something more beautiful, more romantic than that word. The story I read was of a King who fell in love, fell in love with a woman who was of low birth but she was the most beautiful woman in the realm, beautiful enough to capture the heart of her monarch. The legend is that John was a bad king, so bad that only the cathedral here would accept him and even then he had to be dressed in a priest's robes so as to creep into heaven past St Peter. The real story is that he chose to be buried here, he rejected Westminster Abbey so that he could be buried here by his family, where they could come and place flowers on his tomb."

Fitzroy waited for a time as if he had thought that no one knew that story outside of these walls. Then solemnly he replied, "and we still do when I cross the river. King John could never have been buried in Westminster Abbey that last resting place of devils and dictators. If they would have buried him inside that satanic place his bones would have risen up and walked out of there, and sort cleaner soil. "A darkness crossed his face, King John had been wronged and it was a knife which constantly turned within him, not a large knife like the death of his sons, it was smaller like a needle, but it wasn't the only one.

"Your line is direct from King John to now, our King cannot say that," Donald tried to lure out the rest of what was in his head.

"Yes but the throne of England is not for bastards either," Fitzroy replied as Matilda entered and   he looked at Donald before his head sunk, "sorry to use such a word my lady."

Matilda shrugged, "that is alright."

"You used it Fitzroy," Donald replied, "you didn't misuse it. Matilda's not from London anyway, where is it that you are from again Matilda?"

"Rochester," she replied.

Donald smiled, "that's right Fitzroy Rochester, you ever heard of it?"

"Yes I've heard of Roach Chester," Fitzroy replied.

"A noble cathedral city," Donald retorted.

"It's close enough to London to smell the stench from it, it " Fitzroy spat, hatred swirling in his eyes, hatred enough to make Donald afraid, and he didn't scare easily.

A shrill sound then rang out sounding like a horse; Matilda gripped the table, "what is that?"

Fitzroy chuckled, "that is a sound that you do not hear in Roach Chester that will be the animals, quarrelling amongst themselves."

"Do they fight?" Matilda asked.

"Oh all animals fight my lady even those who eat grass. They have to thin their own numbers, sometimes I go out and find they have killed one of their own in the night, and I feed it to the pigs. Maybe they have cornered a fox and are dealing with it."

"Or maybe a person," Donald smiled.

But his smile fell as Fitzroy nodded, "maybe if anyone is stupid enough to enter the courtyard, the night is their time my Lord. In the day I can control them but at night even I would have problems, especially if they have already scented blood."

Donald then leant forwards, "don't you find inbreeding a problem?"

Fitzroy looked up, "what do you mean?"

"Well how many are there of them? Half a dozen, it's a limited gene pool."

"What's that?" Fitzroy spat back.

Donald leant forwards and looked Fitzroy keen in the eye, "inbreeding! It's bad for animals," he paused, "and people." He then drew back and watched Fitzroy's face twitch with anger and he chuckled silently.

"What do you mean?"

"Well with the same genes over and over again the animals can't help but get weaker and weaker," Donald countered.

"Huh! Nonsense, why do not ever see a black man in the royal family then?!" Fitzroy snapped.

"What do you mean?"

"Well if different blood was good then they would marry blacks and Indians and everyone, but the Kings and Queens of Europe believe in keeping their blood pure," Fitzroy replied.

"And it meant that the heir to the Russian throne was sick," Donald replied, "and it ultimately lead to the downfall of the whole family and of Russia itself!"

"Royal blood is not the same as normal blood," Fitzroy protested.

Donald laughed, "why is it blue or something?"

"No royal blood is not like the blood of us peasants, it is a blood that cannot be mixed with just any other type of blood," Fitzroy replied.

Donald laughed, Fitzroy was obviously not use having anyone disagree or argue with him, how many hours had he sat here and espoused his views to only his wife and the four walls? Donald smiled and replied softly, "I'm sure the doctors would argue with that."

"Ah! What do they know?" Fitzroy roared and then looked down into the cloudy gold of his tankard, "so what about you my Lord? I do not know your surname."

"Pembridge, Donald Pembridge, that is my name. No Lord or Sir, just plain Donald Pembridge, so you see Fitzroy my blood is of that common red variety."

Fitzroy nodded and seemed to feel sorry for him, a man so upright and noble but just a plain mister , no better than him in fact. "Well now you have a title my Lord, you are the Lord of Holt Castle, and that is as noble as any dukedom or earldom."

Donald smiled, "might be a slight exaggeration."

Fitzroy was about to explode into a big speech but even he at this stage knew that he was being mocked and let it rest at that.

Donald looked into the fire that Mrs Fitzroy stoked, and saw the past burning, "my family had their own castle once in the far corner of Herefordshire, in that land that slides down into Monmouthshire, a place which is neither Wales or England. My blood traces back to the times of the kingdom of Archenfield, a tiny Welsh kingdom which only survived the English invasion by selling out their brothers further west."

"How do you mean?" Fitzroy edged forwards.

"We saw the English advance, we saw the villages burning in the distance, we saw the people who escaped stream past us as fast as they could, their faces white with fear. Our men gathered together, a few hundred souls, farm hands, old men and the like, hardly an army at all, and you know what they did?"

Fitzroy shook his head, "no."

Donald smiled, "they sent the oldest man amongst them, a man too old to ride even, so he had to walk. Anyway they sent the oldest man in Archenfield out to tell the English that they would have safe passage onto attack the other Welsh if only they would leave them be. The English of course despised my ancestors, but they respected the courage of the old man to walk out alone to face a people who had murdered and pillaged their way across the land, because he never shook or showed any nerves. They didn't think that to a man of that age death was of no importance anyway, in fact it could be a blessing. They replied they only fought with proper men and not cowards and they sent the old man back with the message that the land would be left in peace. So we preserved our Welsh ways until the last century when the modern world came to the Golden Valley and swept away the last of the old tongue." Donald gazed into the fire, "my family has lived there since the days of the old kingdom, since the time of the Romans! They saw the English keep their word and the Archenfielders were untouched as the great war parties passed their land to pillage the Welsh and to bring them to English slavery. Then the Normans came and the noble kingdom was swept into history divided between the English shires of Hereford and Monmouth. My family lost their old Welsh name of Mabyarth, 'son of the bear' and took the name Pembridge, we withstood the Normans as we withstood the Saxons before them." He then slowly rose to his feet, "now if you could excuse me for a moment."

Donald went out and they heard the creak of the door as he walked out to the toilet. Fitzroy looked into the fire as if lost in those days of Saxons and Normans, and he nodded, before slowly muttering, "what a load of shit."

Even Matilda sniggered as Mrs Fitzroy chided him, "you shouldn't be like that dear!"

"Well who wants to listen to all that nonsense of Saxons and Normans and all that?" Fitzroy grunted.

"It is good to know your family history," Mrs Fitzroy countered.

"Not if it is coming out of the book of Herefordshire and Monmouthshire it isn't!" He replied.

"What is wrong with those counties?" Matila asked innocently.

Fitzroy's eyes then rounded like an old boar about to mate, "well he said it himself! They are half Welsh places hardly English at all! Especially if you go deep into Monmouthshire, I mean far beyond Monmouth itself, which is almost a civilized place. Keep going on that road and you will see villages with strange names that only a crazy man could pronounce and you hear their accents change, from the way people speak around here to their nasty Welsh way." Even the word Welsh felt unpleasant on his lips and he had to spit it out quickly.

He was going to say more when they all heard the flush of the toilet and the creak of the door as Donald came back inside again, Matilda leant forwards as Donald entered, "so what became of your family?"

Donald sat down and shrugged, "they lost it all in a game of cards."

"A game of cards?" She asked.

He nodded slowly, "yes a game of cards. Land which had been in my family since the time of the Romans was lost over a Jack of Clubs." He laughed, "you see my father was a gambler, he was addicted to it, as a Scotsman likes his whisky. He was never contented with his little castle, he wanted to be like the Dudleys of Whitley Court, he watched that palace be built and he craved for that kind of wealth. Everything he did failed and so he would risk everything on the turn of a card, that card would make the Pembridges rich and important or would ruin us. It ruined us." Donald held up his hands and shrugged, but there was real bitterness there. He shouldn't be working for anyone but sat down with them drinking tea like an equal. "So you see my dear Fitzroy, we are all workers now, all members of the proletariat here."

"Yes my Lord," Fitzroy replied but then glanced at his wife that was one of those new Bolshevik words, he didn't know what it meant but he knew Bolshevik when it was being spoken.

Chapter Four: The shadows of Dunstall Common

Night set deep in over Holt, pouring into every corner, masking the woods in a cloak of black. Matilda looked out from her room down onto the river, even that was gone, there was no moon, it was buried behind a wall of cloud. She was not use to such darkness; she had never been outside the city before where every street had lines of flickering gas lamps, like friendly forest spirits sending out a glow into the streets below. This place to her eyes was black, dead; there was nothing here once the sun went down. The floor boards creaked, and it seemed that until the early hours the Fitzroys were creeping around the place, or maybe it was her imagination. She was almost glad of the baby's company now, at least it was someone to hold onto, but she knew that if they came for her a baby couldn't save her.

Morning broke over Holt Castle and Matilda found that she had slept a little, she jolted and looked down to her side where the baby was asleep as well, hell she didn't even know her name. The sunlight poured over the old church to reach the castle before tingeing red the river a salmon pink. Matilda headed over to the window and looked down into it, now she regretted ever having come here, it was better to be poor than cursed.

Despite their late night floor board creaking the Fitzroys were up early and the husband was coaching the beasts back to their pen with bits of what looked like dead horse, they looked passive enough with their heads sunk and nodding dazedly, It was evident though in their dark eyes that they were only biding their time until they would turn on him and rip him apart. "We must keep you locked up now," Fitzroy chuckled, "now that we have visitors staying with us from London," and with the mention of that city he spat out a long line of flem. When the last one was locked up in his cage Fitzroy looked into the eyes of one of them, they were his children now.

Matilda edged out of her room with the baby in her arms and lightly tip toed down the stairs, the front door had been left partly open and a gust of cold air and leaves entered uninvited. Slowly she stepped towards it and peered out into the courtyard where Mrs Fitzroy was hurrying herself out of the gate. Where could she be going, it couldn't be past seven? Matilda peered around the edge of the door when she jolted as Fitzroy stepped out in front of her, "is anything wrong?"

Matilda shook her head, "no, just wondering where your wife is going? It is early."

Fitzroy's face flashed with anger at Matilda's rudeness, "yes."

"Yes what?"

Fitzroy smiled, "yes it is early." Fitzroy's eyes lingered in hers for a moment before he brushed past her. One yelp from the animals made Matilda kick the door closed quickly. Fitzroy shuffled into the back and started cursing to himself; Matilda knew he was cursing her. Her eyes then sank to the baby, maybe Fitzroy would tell her something, a hint, a clue, she told herself that she was better off not asking questions, and yet she had to find out. As quietly as she could she entered the kitchen, above the sink there hung the portraits of their two sons, still in their uniforms as they would be forever. There had always been wars but in the past they took one son, the youngest usually, and they left the elder to do their parent's bidding. The new twentieth century states though wanted everything, not just one son, but both, and if you had six they wanted all of them and they would return them to you dead. Fitzroy knew she was there but pretended he never and let her get close and let her whisper: "Mr Fitzroy?"

His eyes rounded on her and she saw them swell with tears, "what is it my lady?"

"'Look, I don't know what all this is, but you do don't you? You know what's going on here."

Fitzroy smiled ironically, "do I my lady?"

Matilda stepped back, "you must do."

Fitzroy shook his head, "it takes years to understand what is going on, and some people live their whole lives and still don't get it."

Matilda tried again, "where was your wife going?"

Fitzroy's face hardened, "that is none of your concern my lady."

"I think it is," she argued.

Fitzroy ignored her, "We are here to help you but we have our private doings as well and they are none of your concern."

"Where did she go?" Matilda persisted.

"Who?" Fitzroy replied.

"Your wife, where did she go?" Matilda asked.

"That is not your business," Fitzroy then replied.

Matilda sighed and gave up,she was about to turn around when he called her back, "Miss Matilda, how well do you know the Lord Donald?"

She shrugged, "I know him no better than I know you. I met him yesterday in London, at Paddington, he was with the baby, and together we travelled up here. In that two hours or so though he hardly spoke just looked out of the window at the countryside passing by."

Fitzroy nodded, "because he will never see it again."

"What do you mean?"

Fitzroy ignored her, "does he ever speak about Lenin?"

"Who?"

Fitzroy smiled, "he spent some of the war years in Russia."

"Did he?" She replied, "why don't you ask him?"

Fitzroy smiled, "it is just this baby is very important, if she should fall into the hands of the enemy then it could cause a great scandal."

She frowned, "but the enemy has been defeated, there is no enemy now."

Fitzroy smiled broadly at her naivety, "there is always another enemy Matilda, there is always another enemy. I mean the Kaiser was the King's cousin, but he was still planning to kill him, kill him, his family, all of us here, he was crazy, a madman. Well miss, if you can't trust your own cousin who can you trust? I mean who is this man? I know his name is Donald Pembridge but what else do we know? I mean where does he come from? No-one knows who he is! We received no word that you were coming either!" He hissed and then looked towards the door incase Donald was there.

"But the whole place is so well prepared," she argued.

"It has been well prepared for a century."

"How long have you been here?"

Fitzroy looked her sternly in the eye, "since the time of good King John my family has been here. I was born here my lady; I have never lived anywhere else. There has been no child born for a century, now we have one," he then leant forwards and peered at the baby's face before nodding slowly, "yes that looks like one of them."

Matilda looked at the baby's face and then up at him, "who? A Romanov?"

Fitzroy then looked up at Matilda with a broad grin, "you know this baby could bring down an Empire."

"What do you mean?"

Fitzroy drew back, and his taunting eyes laughed, "the less you know Miss the better." He then stared at her, long past the time it was not polite to. Matilda turned and went back to the stairs. Fitzroy nodded, maybe she didn't know anything or maybe she was just a good actress, he liked to think he could smell a Bolshevik like he could smell a Hanoverian rat.

Of course Matilda didn't know how back to the time of good King John was but between Fitzroy and Donald she knew who seemed to be the most 'normal,' if that word could still be used since the war. Lightly she headed to Donald's room and tapped on the door. A thump came from the other side of it as Donald's foot hit the floor, he had back there in hell, I knew that when Matilda told me because I had woken like that so many times before, with my hands around a German's throat, or in some hole with the explosions getting closer to me like an ogre's hammer.

The door slowly opened and Donald's head alone appeared around it, "oh Matilda, what is it?" It was obvious that he hadn't slept much, maybe he had been fighting the war all night, as I sometimes had.

"She's gone out," Matilda hissed.

"Who has gone out?" Donald groaned.

"Mrs Fitzroy, really early."

Donald then drew back, only now was he truly awake and he smiled.

"What is it?" Matilda whispered.

"I knew she would," Donald replied.

"But why, what does it mean?"

"It means they don't trust me," Donald whispered, he then shrugged, "I don't blame them, after all who would? "

Strange thing I never dreamt of the war or any of the strange goings on that day, I dreamt of my wife and I wished I had dreamt of the war because that made me sadder than the war ever could of. When I had met her I had thought that my journey had finished with her that I had found love, or maybe that is a lie I was never in love with her. It was more a dependency, a drug I was now getting withdrawal symptoms from.

Dunstall common lies nine miles beyond Worcester, a narrow road cut it in half, rising up above that road was the county's other castle, but it owed more to hobbits than Normans. It was a fantasy with a rounded tower rising up above what looked like a ruined church. Even from a distance it looked like insanity, more a tower of Babel, built to escape the shit realities of this world than any defense against rebellious Saxons. When you got closer though you saw straight through it, it hadn't been built out of the huge boulders that a proper castle would be made out of, instead small pieces of stone had some how been cemented together making it look more like a Scottish crofters hovel than a mighty English castle. As my eyes met it I shook my head in wonderment, so this was where Donald had wanted me to spend the rest of my life, it was hardly anonymous for all his cloak and dagger games, how the hell could a Londoner live in a place like that?

I had arrived there just an hour after I had left Matilda at Holt Castle and had eased my foot on the accelerator as soon as I had seen it, taking it all in as slowly I drove forwards. As if the castle did not draw attention to itself enough the car parked in front of it would make it a tourist attraction. I turned the engine off and shook my head before slowly getting out and looking over the common, a little patch of loneliness in the heart of a densely populated county, there was a village just round a bend in the road but from here it could have been a thousand miles away. For a moment I thought about my son how he would like to run over that grass, didn't he deserve to be here in the sunshine rather than in the smog of London? Then I felt like I had when I had first killed a man, but I shook it from my head as I had back then.

I drew out the key Donald had left in the instructions and fitted it into the door, both were new, very new and the door opened with no moan of un-oiled hinges. I reached inside and my finger tips touched on a light switch, I drew it down, more in hope than expectation, never thinking that it would work, instantly I stepped back as my eyes met an ice cave of unblemished white wash. This place had been recently prepared, you could almost smell the paint still. I should have checked the place out but the kid inside me drew my feet up the winding steps which ended in a trap door. I reached for the bolt and pushed it back before emerging out onto the roof. I then stepped and looked around and marveled. No land is as beautiful as Romania and yet there is a childhood charm to the English countryside. I looked down narrow lanes that cut through apple blossom, villages with their black and white wooden cottages. Oh how I miss that land now, now I am stuck here in Los Angeles, the sunniest but also the darkest city on Earth, if only I could be back there for a week, just to wash away all these shadows. I looked north to where I could make out the tower of Worcester Cathedral, then west to the Malvern Hills where Edward Elgar had ridden his bicycle as he sought inspiration for his music. I imagined walking over those hills; it would be nice to be alone after all that London. To the south Bredon Hill stood, like a lone giant shunned by the other hills that looked more like a place you'd go to shoot yourself, not many people went there, unlike the Malverns. A small dark tower stood on it's summit, my eyes were caught by it and I wondered if it was part of all this, but I never found out what it was and still don't know today. Like Holt Castle it is a place wiped off all the maps. I began to feel happy, maybe it wouldn't be so bad to live here with ten or fifteen miles of countryside between me and Donald and all his sinisterness, then my eyes settled on something.

At first I thought I had imagined it but then I saw it again, at the edge of the common I saw a silhouette, a shadow that slowly became a man the more I looked. The sunlight seemed to glint off something and I knew from my war days what that was, binoculars. A chill ran through me, I was being watched; a good soldier also knew that anyone watching you through binoculars was the enemy. Suddenly the whole fairytale castle crashed down into hell and as the shadow darted back I turned to the trap door and hurtled down the steps like chicken licken running from the falling sky. I burst out, the shadow had gone, I was about to run over to where the shadow had been when I hit something or rather someone. I ran into the arms of a man and the two of us span like battling rugby players into a ditch. I found myself on top of him and drew back to hammer my fist into his face when I saw the uniform of a policeman. Instantly I froze before bending forwards to help him to his feet brushing him down.

The policeman shrugged me off, "you were in a hurry weren't you Sir?"

I stumbled, "yes I thought I saw someone."

"Where?" He snapped.

I pointed over the common, but it was empty, desperately my eyes searched for something, a rabbit or a fox which might explain my mistake but there was nothing and so they fell on the policeman, "did you see nothing?"

The policeman shook his head with a fatherly smile, "no Sir."

My head sunk.

"You've just moved in here have you Sir?"

"Yes yesterday."

He looked over the tower, "this place has been empty for a long, long time."

My eyes were still searching the long grass, "has it?"

"I could never find out who owned it," the policeman added, "have you bought it?"

Then my eyes turned on him, he looked like a typical rosy cheeked country bobby, but he was still a policeman and I had just driven him into a ditch, his wife would spend hours sponging that uniform and yet he seemed to have forgotten about that already. Maybe the Worcestershire police were different to the ones in London, I thought but then I knew police are always police whether in Worcester, London or Kuala Lumpur, they were always the same jumped up little Napoleons, so how could this man be so different? "No, I am just looking after it. Excuse me, but what is your name?"

"Oh –er Defford, PC Defford," he then tipped his forelock and bent his knees slightly like he was in some Gilbert and Sullivan opera, I half expected him to start singing, "and what is your name Sir?"

"Simmonds, Charlie Simmonds," I replied and then looked down at the hand he offered before shaking it. Looking into his eyes I could see they were hiding something, the smile wavered looking as if it would fall at any moment. If he hadn't seen the shadow it must be because he was the shadow, there was a bulge inside his jacket that looked binocular size, and then there was the jacket itself, despite the mud it looked too crisp, too new, no threads of stitching coming away. It didn't quite look like the police uniforms I had seen; maybe they were different up here.

"You from London are you Sir?"

I nodded, "yes, what of it?"

His eyes followed mine as I examined his uniform and he drew back a bit, "just like to know the people who live on my beat, so you don't know who owns this place?"

"No," I replied like a challenge, "it all goes through an agent."

"And who might he be?"

I looked at him and decided it was time to end the charade, "is there anything wrong Constable?"

"No Sir," Defford sighed knowing that he wasn't going to get anything more out of me, then we looked at each other, we both knew and we knew that the other knew. Now the fear was in his face, "well I'd best be on my way."

"Yes I think that you better had," I replied. Defford looked away and then clumsily walked over to where he had left his bike propped up against a tree, like the uniform the bike was brand new. I watched him push the bike up and climb onto it before rolling down the slight bank towards the village unsteadily, it was obvious that he didn't do much cycling; it was only when he had gone someway before he started to struggle with the pedals. I watched him, he knew I was watching him, if this had been the war I would have shot him there and then and let people judge the corpse later. The minute he was out of sight I turned towards the tower and locked it's door before hurrying down towards the village.

Earl's Croome is an instantly forgettable place, the sleepiest of all sleepy villages. I came across a copy of 'the King's England: Worcestershire' in a second hand shop here some months ago, it says something about a 19th century tower sticking out of a Norman church, they did well to get three paragraphs out of this place, because I couldn't. I drew near the first people I saw, two old housewives with nothing better to do but gossip, they had seen me through the corner of their eyes but pretended that they hadn't as I neared. I could see that they were hoping that I wouldn't come over and their faces sunk as I cleared my throat:

"Excuse me ladies."

"Good morning," one replied, the other just faintly smiled, this was old England and married women did not just give away their greetings.

"I've just moved into the tower," I began and watched the surprise wash over their faces.

"Oh that's been empty for years," the one who hadn't wanted to speak exclaimed.

I nodded and smiled weakly, "yes it has."

"We thought something was going on though, I said to you didn't I Mavis, when them men came out to work in it, I said something was going to happen there," she continued.

"Oh it's been empty for years though Deidre," Mavis agreed, "my mother said she could never remember anyone living there."

They were beginning to irritate me, and so I trod onto their conversation, "I just had a policeman come out there, he said he was called Defford, do you know him?"

Mavis frowned, "Defford? No, the only policeman around here is PC Bailey, we calls him Bill Bailey, you know like the song?"

I nodded, "yes."

"Unless he meant he came from Defford," Mavis cut in as if she had just solved a great mathematical equation, "that's a village a couple of miles up the road."

"Yes but there's no police station there," Deidre argued.

"Bill Bailey isn't from Defford anyway, he's from Upton, he comes up from there on his bike," Mavis replied.

I nodded, "thank you ladies." I then turned, my blood iced, he had to be false, Defford was the first name which had come into his head, no doubt he had passed through the place on the way down.

Their eyes followed me as I walked back towards the tower and I heard Mavis grumble, "well he's a strange one isn't he?"

"But dishy," Deidre giggled.

"Don't let your husband hear you say that," Mavis warned, and then the laughter stopped.

I walked back to the tower; suddenly London didn't seem such a bad place. It was one thing to be involved in something mysterious and maybe illegal if it was a secret, but obviously someone already knew. Maybe *Defford* was a policeman, if so he wasn't the usual country bobby; he was something higher up than that, higher up than anything in Worcester. I knew the sort, after all hadn't I been in the cloak and dagger business myself in Romania? One thing for sure was that this place was now compromised; whoever Donald wanted to keep the secret from now knew. The tower now looked more like a tomb, I had to get out.

I drove off down the narrow track, past Mavis and Deidre who were still gossiping, God only knew what state their houses were in, there wasn't anyone much else around in the village, I passed an old man who didn't seem to see me, he didn't see anyone anymore. A few hundred yards out of the village I came upon the main road from Upton to Pershore road . There weren't many cars on the roads back in those days, not like the Los Angeles of outside, even at this hour I can hear the cars passing. I should have been able to hit the gas as soon as I got onto that main road, but there were too many horse and carts back then, meandering along like in some Constable painting. As I pulled off I looked in my rear view mirror and I saw a car on the verge and I saw it pull off too, I wiped my arm across my forehead, I was back in Romania, being tailed by German agents, back in the early days when we had been followed everywhere, and I had slept with a pistol under my pillow. The car had been perched up a hill where it could see the tower and see which way I was going, and then it had parked here, like a lion waiting for a zebra to emerge from the bush.

I drove down towards Upton and tried to organize my thoughts. Back in Romania Donald had always been with me, sat in the back seat looking completely calm, seldom had he looked back. 'But if the Germans have orders to kill us?' I asked.

'Then we must kill them first,' Donald had replied calmly.

Now I was my own, I crossed the main Worcester to Gloucester road hoping the car would take a left or right there but of course it followed me straight across and down the steep bank towards the river. I tried not to look back too much but I had to now and again because you never knew when they would try some move to try to force me off the road. Instead of building their town on top of that steep bank the wise founding fathers of the town had built their town right next to the country's grandest river and so it flooded every year without fail, it was as regular as Christmas or New Year's. If I was expected a big metropolis to lose my pursuers in I was quickly disappointed, there were villages bigger than this place, I made a sharp right and headed towards Worcester along the west bank, I would have better to take the other road, few cars travelled this way. Of course my pursuer took the same way, I wasn't paranoid, what were the chances that of all the other ways he could have taken he would take the same way as me? It was possible of course, but not likely. This road would take us to Worcester but miss most of it, it would only take us through the west or 'Welsh' side of St John's, maybe we would part company there, again I doubted that. Whatever it was that I had gotten myself involved in it was better if I got myself uninvolved because something told me that someone usually got killed in this kind of thing, and it was usually the guy at the bottom.

It was a lonely road that was only kept in order for when the road on the other side of the river got flooded, and there was only two cars on it, mine and my pursuer, I weaved past the odd cart that plodded past like a huge sloth and I prayed that some idiot herding sheep or cattle hadn't blocked the road past the next bend. No one much ever came down the road from Worcester because Upton was a nothing place and beyond Upton the road got lost. My pursuer just kept his same distance, varying not one foot. Maybe I should go to Worcester, after all Donald wouldn't want me leading them back to him. Maybe I should head to the real police, but what if the baby was kidnapped? Maybe Donald was waiting for a big ransom and I would be looking towards spending a long time in jail. Maybe Defford had been a real policeman, maybe they were behind me, and maybe I should just stop now and confess everything, but what if Donald was still working for the same old people, the biggest bandits of all: the British government?

There were a few villages I passed: Hanley Castle, where the castle had long since been swept away leaving only ditches, Callow End and then Powick. Powick was a nothing place you could drive through without noticing, but it was here where the English civil war had begun and ended. The church tower was still pock marked from the last great battle of Worcester, it was from there that King Charles II had stood and watched his army get crushed by Cromwell's new model republicans, the river Teme had run red that day. What Englishman these days really knows about Cromwell? Who knows about his ideas and ideals, we've lived under so many centuries of royalist propa ganda, but for a time England had been different, that's all I knew, there had been no King or Queen, I didn't know if it had been better or worse. Certainly Cromwell had put the Irish in their place I knew that, our King and his parliament had just caved into them, after defeating the Kaiser's mighty war machine they had been made to look like buffoons by a pack of Irish bandits. Thousands had died in those fields, it was hard to know now what they had died for, but then it is like that for most wars. I passed Powick Bridge where the English civil war had begun in a minor skirmish. A new bridge had been built now, so I glanced at the old one, to me back then it was like a hundred other old bridges across the country, I have read a lot since then, I have had time to.

Beyond the Teme Worcester started to encroach and I breathed a sigh of relief. I looked down at the passenger seat, certainly I would have been happier if there had been a pistol there, I felt naked without one. The road forked and I took the right fork which was new houses on one side and fields on the other, from there the cathedral could be seen in all it's might, my eyes flitted to the rear view mirror, they knew what they were doing, it wasn't so easy to tail someone. When I had tailed someone in Romania though I had tried to make sure that they couldn't see me, my pursuers weren't bothered about that. Why didn't I just pull over? After all this wasn't the war, they wouldn't kill me or beat me up. I sank down a hill and the pastureland receded to a cricket field and I came to a crossroads. The car slowed behind me, my eyes flitted over to the doors to make sure that I had locked them, then it was barely amber when I pulled off. St John's old church watched perplexed as I sped off past the cripple's gate, I looked in the mirror feverously, and my pursuers had down the same. I drove through the city as if it was Lisbon and I couldn't get out of it quick enough. I got to the place where both signs said 'Tenbury Wells' and I swerved left, the Martley Road, Donald wouldn't want me to take these people anywhere near him. I looked at the petrol situation, I had enough to get there, wherever I was going.` The best thing I could do now was go to Tenbury Wells and buy something from a shop there and then head back and pretend that nothing was out of the ordinary, but then who would drive past Worcester to go to there and buy something? The car behind me was almost driving in my tyre tracks obeying every bend, every swerve.

Martley itself was a sizeable enough village, there was enough people milling about, I could have just parked in front of the pub, run inside and shouted that the Germans after me, maybe that would just me a place in the local nuthouse, there were certainly enough people doing that these days. I wish I could have admired the view because it got more and more lovely, the Teme Valley itself looks like something from a fairy tale. Still I dream of buying a house there, you can almost feel your soul dying here. A steep bank lead down to the river and an even steeper one leads out of it. I looked down at my leg, it was shaking and I was beginning to get that old sickness in my stomach again and I prayed that this car didn't break down. As I pressed the accelerator and climbed up the bank towards Clifton, a smile rose on my face, I knew what I should do. God knows why I worry so much, I don't enjoy life that much anyway to worry about losing it anyway, but then these guys normally torture you first. I thought about my son though, he would never know me; maybe it was better that way.

Tenbury Wells itself is a forgettable place, hardly worth the journey, no castle or abbey to buy a postcard of, not many shops to sell it either. There was however ironmongers and that is what I wanted, so I pulled up before it and glanced back. The following car pulled up nearly on a bend, good I nodded and got out. I could almost hear their thoughts; this had to be the place, the place where we were hiding the baby. There was the usual collection of rustic folk in the street, because this was no town like Worcester; this was a piece of a town dumped right into the middle of their world of sheep dips and bad cyder. I went into the shop and came out after a few minutes and then walked calmly down towards their car as if I had a portion of chips and wished to offer them one. I grinned to myself as I watched it's occupants disappear behind their newspapers, that is just what I wanted, they never saw it as I sank to my knees and threw a handful of tacks under one of their back wheels, I then rose quickly to my feet and entered a butcher's shop. Inside the shop I could see them look round for me in panic and then calm as they saw.

"What would you like Sir?" The butcher asked.

"Sausages please, that line there will be nice please," I replied.

"You're not from around here are you Sir?" He smiled.

"No I am not."

"Where are you from then?" He asked drawing out the tray of sausages.

"London."

"London!" He exclaimed as if the King himself had just entered his shop, "what ever brings you up here then?"

"Your sausages I have heard that they are very good."
The butcher almost feinted such was the shock on his face, he wrapped them up and handed with his eyes and mouth still gaping open, he tried to refuse payment but I insisted before striding out with my prized sausages. The butcher stepped out onto the pavement behind me as I walked down towards my car, and as he saw it he scratched his head, he had never seen such a car, it only confirmed what I had said, I was from London. As I looked in the rear view mirror I giggled at the butcher and then I pulled off and openly laughed as my pursuers pulled off and immediately got a flat. Yes! It had worked, God knows if I had seen it in some film or something or if it was just a moment of inspiration. They tried to carry on but didn't even get as far as the bridge. It was there that the butcher caught up with them.

"That man came all the way from London to buy my sausages!"

The driver just looked at him with a sick face.

I drove over the river Teme again and then turned right and took the other road back to Worcester. It seemed crazy that something so simple could work so easily, they would change the wheel but that would take them half an hour and by that time I would be too far away. This road would take me to Holt, I had to talk to Donald before I carried on with anything. I could still feel my leg tremble, I had not been this scared since the war, I had almost forgotten what it felt like, of course everyone lives with fear but it is a different kind in civilian life, fear of losing your job, not being able to pay the rent, your wife is cheating...in war you fear is not being alive the next day or hour, or minute. At least now I had a choice, you can't walk away from a trench. I calmed down as I drove along that road which ran between the river and a railway line, I looked at my speed and slowed down, the last thing that I wanted was a crash. Those men could have killed me, God only knew what they had wanted, I had gotten away with it now I should return the car to Donald and walk away.

I passed three villages which I can scarcely remember, Rochford, Lindridge and Knighton-on-Teme, no doubt the 'on-Teme' bit was to stop people mixing it up with the town in the Welsh borders, but that was also on the Teme, so there was no logic there unless there was another Knighton in Worcestershire somewhere. I remember Abberley, climbing up it's great hill and gazing up at the great clock tower, there was no tower there when Henry IV had stationed his armies there as they faced Owen Glendower's band of Welsh and French marauders through this bramble covered land. On the other side of the hill there was a hotel and people were gathered outside it, they didn't look like the usual village types, something had to be going on there, but I never stopped to find out. They all looked at the car as if they had expected it to stop as if one of their friends should have been inside it. The greatest shock on the road was at Whitley because there I passed a palace, I know that word is used freely by writers, but it truly was, like the home of the Tsars had fallen out of Russia and landed in rural England. A gold dome cupola rose from it, which was a church it's masters had built, inside that church folk say that it is as close as you can get to Rome without going there, such is the gold and paintings which cover it's walls and ceilings, and it's sculptures that even the Caesars would envy. Of course I never saw it and never will now I guess. Holt was not that far from Whitley and the castle did look pitiful next to it.

It was nearly eleven before the Lord of Holt Castle came down the stairs dressed impeccably and an aroma of expensive fragrance drifted over the dining room, causing Fitzroy's head to jerk round thinking some rich lady had entered. He shook his head when he saw that it was only Donald smelling like a Parisian pimp, but he couldn't meet his eyes today. Donald smirked, he would be no good in court they would hang him for sure, then he remembered that Romanian they had caught working for the Germans and his face darkened again, his eyes had been like that, before he had killed him. As Donald sat down Fitzroy placed the bacon and eggs in front of him and prayed that he never mentioned his wife, "that looks nice Fitzroy."

"Thank you Sir."

"Didn't know you could cook."

Fitzroy's face warmed, "it's only bacon and eggs you don't need to be no cook to do that."

Donald then leant forwards, "I was wondering about the church Fitzroy."

"The Church Sir?" Fitzroy turned surprised, "are you a church man then Sir?"

"Yes of course," Donald chuckled, "why wouldn't I be?"

"Oh I don't know Sir, you are a modern man with modern ways."

Donald nodded, "thank you Fitzroy, but they haven't disproved God yet have they?"

'But in Russia," Fitzroy continued.

Donald's smile then broadened, "what has Russia got to do with me?"

"I don't know Sir, well you were there weren't you?"

Donald nodded, "I've been to a lot of places Fitzroy. I would like to see inside the church."

Fitzroy hesitated, "a lot of churches were burnt down in Russia, left just ashes they were."

Donald nodded, "the wooden ones yes they were, so?"

Fitzroy wanted to continue the argument but could see it was pointless. "Yes you can see the church Sir, it is the same as it ever was, and little has changed since the Normans."

"Maybe we will need a new vicar," Donald mused.

Fitzroy's eyebrows rose, "a vicar?! There has not been a priest here in a century. Whenever I feel the need for a good church service I cross the river to Ombersley."

Donald nodded, "yes quite, but Ombersley will not do for this child, we will need our own reverend, a man who will come here and never leave, you can see that can't you Fitzroy?"

"Yes I can see that Sir, but what kind of man would do that?"

"An old man who wishes to be alone, there are such men even in the English church," Donald smiled.

"That sounds like the kind of man with a past, with some kind of secret," Fitzroy grunted.

"Oh we all have secrets Fitzroy," Donald toyed with him, "the child will need to be christened."

"And maybe married one day," Fitzroy added.

A pained expression crossed Donald's face, "well we will see about that, maybe one day." Fitzroy was about to turn away when Donald added, "Fitzroy why do you use the word priest?"

"Sorry Sir?"

"Well I know the Church of England is a very broad church, but it is not a word many English people use, I mean it is more for Papists and our friends in the east," Donald smiled.

"Oh dear Sir have I been using the wrong word again?" Fitzroy shrugged as if he had had enough of games, he headed over to a drawer and pulled it open before slapping a huge and ancient key on the table. "That is the key to the church my Lord, it is yours to enter at any time."

"Thank you Fitzroy, I will try not to burn it down."

Donald took it and after he had finished his breakfast, he left his plate for the scowling Fitzroy to take before he headed out to the church as I drove up the old muddy track and then stopped in front of the gate before sounding my horn. It was a different Simmonds who got out of the car, no longer humble, wanting to keep his job, no job was this much trouble and I didn't mind losing it. Donald came out, his face bubbling with irritation, "you were told only to come here if instructed!"

I nodded, "yes."

"Then why are you here?"
I folded my arms, "tell me why is that tower you gave me to live in being watched?"

Donald's face then fell and blanched, "what? Are you sure?"

"Yes, a policeman showed up there today, only he wasn't a policeman," I replied.

"Are you sure?" he repeated.

"Then he followed me all the way to Tenbury Wells," I added.

Donald then nodded and cursed, "you'd best come inside and tell me the whole story." He then growled for Fitzroy to come and open the gate. He then strutted about and cursed over and over again.

I entered the house and met Mrs Fitzroy's unpleasing face, "oh why are you back so soon Mr, oh what was-"

"Simmonds," I replied and sat down at the head of the table.

"I'll put some tea on for you Mr –er."

"Simmonds," I repeated, "and you'd better make that tea a large brandy instead."

Then Donald entered with Fitzroy close behind him, "then they know."

"Make it two brandies, or maybe three," I quipped.

"I don't know," Donald snapped.

"Somebody knows!" Fitzroy retorted.

"They know some but not all," Donald agreed, "and we don't even know who they are,"

"What do you mean?" Fitzroy grunted.

"They know about Dunstall Castle but not here they wouldn't have followed Simmonds if they would have known," Donald concluded his eyes then fell on me, "you lost them didn't you? I mean you lost them in Tenbury Wells didn't you?"

I nodded, "threw tacks under their back wheel, didn't get as far as the bridge before the tyre blew."

Donald laughed, "good show!"

I downed the brandy in one go before my eyes rounded on Donald's as their equals, "look you'd better start being straight with me Donald else you can deal me out of this game now. That baby in there whose is it? Is it, is she kidnapped?"

Matilda edged into the room with the baby in her arms, Donald looked back at her and smiled embarrassed, "what are you talking about?"

"Now whatever's going on here, you know about it, they know about it but I don't, and I reckon that little lady there doesn't," I replied, "now is that baby stolen?"

"Of course not!" Donald roared, "her parents are the ones who sent me away with her!"

Matilda edged closer.

"I may be poor Sir but I am not stupid, I went over the top in 1918 because I would have been shot if I hadn't, not because I thought it was a clever thing to do. Who the hell is going to give their baby to you?"

"What's that meant to mean?" Donald barked.

"Nobody, no parents send their baby away like that," I countered.

"They do if the baby is am embarrassment to them, even people in your poor areas do that don't they Mr Simmonds?" he mocked. "In my experience the poorer the people the more vicious they are."

I ignored his jibe, "what do you mean embarrassment?"

Donald smiled, "the family I am working for cannot bear a scandal, the baby was born out of wedlock," he then looked back at Fitzroy who nodded, endorsing the lie.

"Yes," I nodded and snatched the brandy bottle that had been left in my range and helped myself to another glass. "Those people following me weren't from the *Daily Mail*, I know that, what I don't know is if they were police or not. How do I know that you are not kidnappers?"
Donald smiled and leant back, "look around you Simmonds, this is a thing of centuries not a few days. "

"What do you mean?" I replied.

Donald went back into his shell a little, "you said yourself that the policeman didn't look like a policeman."

"Yes but they could still be working for the government," I countered.

"Yes, yes they could be," Donald conceded, "but we are working for someone even higher."

I leant back arrogantly, "who God?"

"No, the King!"

A silence fell over the room, until I stammered, "but aren't they the same thing?"

"This land, this county will tell you that that isn't true, king and parliament waged war here. The government does things the King knows nothing about and the royal household does things the Prime Minster knows nothing about. There is a degree of independence between the two. "Donald then drew back like he had just laid out a winning hand, "it now all depends who you want to serve your King or your Prime Minister."

"The one appointed by God or the one who was appointed by some dodgy election where most people voted for the other side," Fitzroy added.

No Briton had to think long about that one, "I will serve my King of course, but doesn't the parliament serve the King as well?"

Donald shook his head, "not always, there are things that the King does not want the government to know about." Before I could ask another question Donald went onto his plan, "what we will do is go back to Dunstall and lie in wait for them there."

"That could be dangerous," Fitzroy grunted, "what if they are Bolshevik agents?"

"They could be," Donald agreed, "that is why we will bring two friends with us." With that he walked over to a briefcase and laid it down on the table, opening it and drawing out two revolvers. Fitzroy's eyes broadened like they were crystal balls. Lightly he rested them on the table before looking up at me.

"Are you joking?" I gasped, "I'm not killing anyone, and there is no war now."

Donald smiled weakly, "there is always some war going on somewhere."

"In the war you kill someone and get a medal, even if their friends capture you, you are treated as a captured enemy, not a killer. You kill someone here and you'll get the rope or you'll spend ever sunny summer behind bars, rotting in jail," I replied.

Donald nodded, "I do not want to kill anyone either, I want to know who these people are, I can hardly get them to talk if they are dead can I?" He then looked down at the guns and smiled, "take one."

I hesitated; my eyes drew to Matilda's before I took up one of the guns.

"Just like old times," Donald smiled.

I then looked up at him coldly, "I hope you know what you're doing."

Donald nodded, "I always did didn't I do?"

"No," I replied.

We drove back to Dunstall this time with Donald sat up front next to me, "you don't seem scared," I noted.

"We have both faced death before haven't we?" He replied.

"Yes but I try not to make a habit out of it."

I then looked at him, he was an odd character, but odd characters and run of the mill people like me had both died in the trenches side by side. " We loved our King," I started, "but I doubted our King loved us, at least not as much as we loved him. You don't throw the best of your harvest to the wind."

"I never knew you were so poetic Simmonds," Donald mocked

"We were just necessary to keep them in their palaces," I tried again, " or maybe I'm wrong."

"Maybe we're all wrong Simmonds, it's not just the man in the street, maybe no one knows what's going on, not even the King."

"You know," I started again, "maybe the King should trust his people more, I mean we love him, we would stand by him through anything."

"And maybe your ancestors were amongst those who stood with Cromwell and cut a King's head off," Donald leant back and smiled as if enjoying the countryside. "You know Simmonds sometimes when you start a lie it is alright, but then you have to keep lying and you lie and lie yourself into a deep hole, a hole the size of a canyon."

"You mean the King is a liar?" I whispered.

Donald shifted uncertainly in his seat, "all this began long ago in the times of King John, it is all here because this was a special place for him. He passed this land in love, in love away from all the intrigues of court. Although everyone is now agreed that he was a bad king what he laid in place was seen as wise and so no one has changed it since. I will now tell you what you want to know, if I don't you will imagine libraries of insanity. The child back there in Holt Castle is a challenger to the throne."

I frowned, "which throne?"

"Our throne! The British Empire, Australia, India all of it! If the King's enemies here or abroad know about this child's existence it will not just cause a scandal but a crisis. We may have to kill the child if our enemies find out about her!"

I almost stopped the car, "kill a baby!"

Donald drew back, "worse things have been done in the name of the King."

Chapter Five: Donald the Demon

Matilda told me later that she watched Donald and I leave like the last members of humanity leave the zoo, now she was alone with Fitzroys and the other strange animals outside. Somehow they seemed to mirror each other, the dogs that weren't dogs and the people who weren't quite human. Maybe they had had their own company too much and for too long, this was like their desert island. She thought about the baby and then her own baby, in a way she had been lucky that he had died, she wasn't married and the father wouldn't marry her in a million years, and yet there was a deep sorrow gnawing at her, a yearning to be a mother and the little hands which touched her felt foreign alien, like a cuckoo chick snuggling up to it's foster mother. The baby's eyes though settled on her as the only mother she had ever known and she would love that child after a while, but hate herself for doing so. Matilda was about to return to her room when her eyes fell on Fitzroy:

"I don't like it."

"I'm sorry," Matilda asked, "you don't like what?"

"How did they find out about Dunstall?" Fitzroy asked, "there must be a rat somewhere amongst us."

"Well it wasn't me!" Matilda protested.

Fitzroy looked at her suspiciously for a long, lingering time before grunting with a nod: "I knows that, I mean you ain't been anywhere to talk to anyone, but I ain't sure about your Mister Donald, I mean I have never heard of no Pembridge family and I should have if they are being brought into this."

"I'm sure you can trust him," Matilda replied.

Fitzroy looked at her, she felt like he was undressing with his eyes but not in a sexual way more in revulsion, "oh that's what you thinks is it? You can trust him, well I can't! I don't know if the family have sent him or someone else has!"

"What family?"

Fitzroy ignored her, "he knows who I am, we have been here at Holt since King John sent us here, everyone knows who we are, but I have never heard of him. No one ever found out about us before he came here now we're famous."

"I wouldn't go that far," Matilda argued.

"He's either a traitor or a fool and either thing ain't no good for us here."

Matilda looked away, "well really it isn't my place to ask questions, I am getting paid, it is a job for me and that is that."

"Your throat will be slit as surely as mine if the Bolsheviks arrive here," Fitzroy warned.

"I doubt that will happen," Matilda answered.

"Are you stupid girl?!" Fitzroy roared, "didn't you hear what he said, this is the King's business, look what those bastards did to the King's cousin and his family in Russia! I told you what they did didn't I? They killed the lot of them, and they didn't spare the servants neither! I may strike you just as a simple country man, but I have read much about this, and I have listened to the wireless. The devil is driving these people, these Bolsheviks, and he's a bastard who never rests," he then paused, "my lady."

"Neither does God," Matilda replied.

"God?" Fitzroy grinned, "we don't see Him much around here, they didn't see him in Russia neither, their King was one for praying too, he use to go to that church with the priests with the big hats. Donald's one of them I can smell it on him."

"One of what?" Matilda asked.

"One of them Bolsheviks," Fitzroy sneered.

She looked away and brushed past him, Fitzroy looked after her, he didn't trust that bitch either, it wasn't natural not to ask questions especially when there were so many to ask. He then dragged the gate back, shutting the outside world out once more.

As Matilda entered the castle she could hear the baby cry and she was about to hurry up to her room when Mrs Fitzroy emerged from the kitchen with the child in her arms, "she's a pretty little thing isn't she?"

"Yes," Matilda hovered, half expecting Mrs Fitzroy to drop the baby and then say 'woops.'

"She will be a heart breaker when she gets older," she added.

"Yes," Matilda smiled uneasily, and drew forwards, lightly taking the baby off her, and nursing her close to her bosom, before looking up at the woman's unpleasing face, "how did you and your husband meet?"

Mrs Fitzroy looked away, and never met Matilda's eyes again, "I came here when I was thirteen, I was an orphan."

"What as a servant?" Matilda asked.

"Yes kind of," she replied, "I was brought in for John."

"I'm sorry?"

Mrs Fitzroy looked away, out over Worcestershire, "his parents knew that he would find it hard to get a girlfriend and that would mean him either mixing with the outsiders in the villages, and you know what those folk are like there, they think we are cursed or something, there is no way they would want their daughters marrying John, so I was brought in to mate with him."

"I'm sorry?" Matilda repeated, thinking that she had heard wrong.

"There was nothing else that could have been done," she then smiled and blushed, "he took some time to rise to the task but when he did he was like a young boar."

Matilda looked at her, to see if she was serious and then felt a revulsion pass through her when she saw that she was.

"Oh he's not much to look at I know that, but he makes up for it in other ways," Mrs Fitzroy smiled.

"Yes I should imagine," Matilda replied.

"What was your husband like?"

"I'm sorry?"

"Well John was saying that you had a man once," her eyes pried into hers.

"I'd rather not say."

"Oh never mind," Mrs Fitzroy mocked, "of course it takes sometime to get used to all the little ways and traditions of this place. I never regret having come here, I never miss the world beyond that hedge."

"But you go out sometimes I mean to Worcester," Matilda argued.

"Yes seldom, but it makes me feel queasy after a while," the old devilment then returned to her eyes, "now what about you my dear?"

"I'm sorry?"

"What became of your husband?"

Matilda looked away, Mrs Fitzroy was close enough for her to feel her hot breath on her neck, "I have never been married."

"Ah," Mrs Fitzroy then drew back and her arched up in a cruel smile, "but the way your breasts are giving off milk you must be pregnant or was pregnant or some such thing."

Matilda pulled her blouse around her bosom, but still she got the impression that they were being inspected.

"Yes I was pregnant once," Matilda admitted.

"Then where is the little nipper?" Mrs Fitzroy asked.

"Dead," Matilda replied coldly. For a moment she was back there, she could see the tiny body, the little hands grasping for air as his mouth opened in silence. I still see her sometimes sit there and think of him, I know she is thinking of him, her eyes are never like that any other time; they are glazed and distant, yearning for the past to change, praying that the baby lives.

"Oh I am sorry my dear, that must have been terrible for you," Mrs Fitzroy was hardly a good actress and Matilda felt like drawing her nails down her face and clawing that hideous hag's mass of wrinkles off, she would like to see her in a bad part of London and see how long that big mouth of her would stay open.

"I think she needs milk,"Matilda replied, nodding down towards the baby.

"Yes we musn't let anything happen to this one," Mrs Fitzroy replied acidly.

As Matilda went upstairs John Fitzroy entered, his eyes followed their guest before turning to his wife, whose expression was the same as his, "so what do you think love?"

Mrs Fitzroy moved forwards and started whispering, "you were right about her, she is some kind of a prostitute. Imagine a baby of royal blood brought up by a scarlet woman! Why it's a bigger scandal than the one we are meant to be hiding."

Fitzroy nodded, "yes my dear, but she is the least of our troubles I reckon. It's that Mr Pembridge that I don't likes, there is something about him that I don't trust, he looks like a pedigree but smells like a fox. I'd like to take a shot gun to all of them if I could."

Mrs Fitzroy laughed, "You're getting to sound like a Bolshevik yourself dear."

I thought of Matilda as we headed through Worcester, I thought of her back there with those that creepy couple, at least I wasn't outnumbered here, it was just me and Donald, and I could get out of the car at anytime. I won't try to make this sound like some great romance though, I thought about a lot of things, I thought about my son, I thought about my wife, I thought about us making love, it seemed so long ago now, almost like they were different people now.

The road south out of Worcester is called the Bath road, God only knew why when most of the people taking that road would have been heading to Gloucester or Bristol, maybe it seemed more gentile for them to say that they were heading to that regency wonderland of Bath to take the waters, maybe it was the lie people in Worcester had once said. In Birmingham there is no Bath road only the Bristol road.

I glanced over to Donald checking the revolvers yet again, how many times had he already done that? There was a time when it stopped being good preparation and became nerves. "How do I know that I am not going to end up dead, Sir?" I asked.

He smiled before looking up, "we're all going to end up dead Simmonds, you know that."

"You know what I mean."

Donald shrugged and looked out onto a line of Victorian mansions; maybe that's why it was the Bath road because the houses were like palaces there, not because it leads to Bath but because it looked like the place. "It's funny you know Simmonds, you went over the top, all those bullets were fired and all they all missed you."

"I guess I must be lucky," I replied.

"It would be strange if after surviving that hell, where thousands no millions died, if after living through that you were killed in a quiet Worcestershire country lane," Donald smiled.

"Stranger things have happened," I replied. "Do you think that the world will ever go back to the way it was, you know before the war?"

"Do you remember what that was like?" he asked.

I shrugged, "kind of, I was only a kid really."

"We were all children before the war, even I was and I was nearly thirty," Donald smiled.

"Before the war the world seemed better," I continued, "maybe the nightmare was always there but we just never knew it."

Donald nodded, "it was like a trap door beneath which a devil lay. Now the door has been opened, we know the devil is there even though the door has closed again."

My eyes returned to him, "so am I going to end up dead? I mean is the bullet going to come from our own side?"

Donald's eyes fell on me, "I can't guarantee anything, they could kill us both, it is a dangerous business that we are involved in."

"A dangerous business that you brought me into," I muttered.

The road carried on out of Worcester into that open country that just waited every year for the Severn to flood. "One thing's for sure Simmonds," Donald mused.

"What's that?" I asked.

"They are planning up another one," Donald smiled.

"Another what?"

"Another war of course," Donald replied matter of factly.

"Who?" I frowned.

"The people who got rich out of the first one, and some people did get very rich out of it. The people who make all those arms, they need another one to keep their factories running."

I shuddered, "at least I'll be too old to fight in the next one."

"Well let's hope you only have daughters then," Donald smiled.

I nodded, "I have a son, but he will never be a soldier."

Donald was going to ask about him but there was something about my expression that told him that it was better not to.

"So where did you find Matilda?" I asked.

Donald smiled, "why do you like her?"

"I'm married," I replied.

"You are married but you don't wear a ring," he smiled.

"It's that kind of marriage," I looked down.

Donald nodded, "yes I understand."

We passed Kempsey which was a big village but didn't seem to have much to show for it, an old church hidden down a lane was about it. Then we climbed up a steep twisting bank at a place called Severn Stoke which looked as if it belonged more in the Carpathians before we reached the top and I saw countryside I knew, there was the Upton to Pershore road. "That's Pershore somewhere over there," Donald noted, "it's a pretty place people say, there's an old abbey there and the river Avon passes by."

I shook my head, "you've got a gun there and you are thinking of picnics."

Donald smiled, "this will all blow over."

"Like the wind over our graves," I muttered.

"You really are turning into a poet Simmonds, I understand a lot of people did that in the trenches, where I was we were too busy fighting to write ditties," Donald mocked.

I never answered that, I turned off the Gloucester road and took the Pershore one, turning off it at a cross where there was written the names of those less fortunate than Donald and myself, I wonder how many poets had been there, their poetry now dead forever. At Earl's Croome the same two women were still there gossiping, I shook my head, "they were there doing that earlier. I bet their houses are as dirty as a rubbish tip, their husbands must clean their houses when they get home from work, and they probably cook their own food as well."

"Yes women these days aren't like they were," Donald agreed.

Then we turned a corner and looked over the tower, truly something which belonged in Narnia, "it's a weird looking thing," I sighed, "who built it?"

"We had it built a few years after the Americans decided to plunge themselves into a republic," Donald replied.

"If this is such a secret that no one knows, then why build a place like this? I mean it's hardly something that people could pass without stopping," I replied before drawing up the car before it, and then gazing up it's mass of small, jagged stones to the quaint turret sticking from it's top.

Donald nodded, "sometimes people let their imaginations get away with them, maybe in those days it was alright, but we live in the days now of the nosey bastard, people who want to discover the countryside around them, that kind of thing." He then cautiously got out, the way he had in Romania, with a gun in both hands and looked around him, "can you see them?"

I shook my head, "no, can you?"

"No, but then if they are any good you won't," he replied.

My eyes then sunk to his pistols, "are you really going to use those things?"

"Haven't you killed before Simmonds, or did you always fire wide when you were in a battle?" Donald mocked, "one of those people who found Jesus in the trenches."

I shook my head, "no I never saw Him there, never saw Him there or anywhere else but this is England and an England at peace, it isn't Jesus who is going to hang if all this goes wrong, let's head back Sir, I mean this has gone far enough."

Donald shook his head, "in the war we shot stable boys from Bavaria and factory workers from Berlin, people innocent of everything except being German. If I shoot anyone today it will be someone plotting against the King. However as I said before, I am not planning to kill anyone, now let's go inside."

As soon as we got inside Donald looked around the room like a great stalk invading another's nest before striding up the spiral of steps, the tower had not been meant for a man as tall as he was and so he bent double as he climbed them. I decided to be more cautious and looked around the place to see if it was the same as when I left it, but then I realized I couldn't remember how I had left it. Donald pushed open the door on the roof before crawling over it. I was about to do the same when he hissed back, "no stand up! I want them to see you, but I do not want them to see me."

I shrugged and smiled slightly, it was all beginning to look like a children's game, I then walked over to the battlements and looked over the countryside casually, "who do you think they are?"

"Well at least they're not Germans," he replied.

"Oh they might be, getting revenge against their old foe," I replied.

"No they have enough problems now, and no money," he rolled over onto his back and held his pistols ready, all I was worried is that one of them might go off by mistake and I might be on the wrong end of it.

"Why is it good that they aren't Germans," I asked.

"Oh Germans are determined, you must have noticed that, they get an order and the order might be stupid and they know it is but they are determined to carry it out, they do things that an Englishman or a Frenchie would mutiny before they did," he replied.

"So how long are we going to be out here?" I sighed.

"As long as it takes."

"Well I hope it doesn't rain then," I smiled.

"Rain isn't too bad, in Russia I saw men who had frozen to death, just hunched there like statues, and they were as hard as bronze as well when you touched them," Donald then looked at me. "You must have passed through Powick yesterday."

"Yes," I grunted, "what of it?"

"What did you think of it? An old church and an old bridge, not much else," Donald smiled.

I nodded, "yes there was a pub I could imagine sitting outside on a sunny day."

"You didn't see the hospital then?" Donald smiled.

"Hospital?"

"Yes you came from Upton, the hospital is on the road that goes up to Malvern. You see Simmonds, say the name Powick to the people of this county and you will see fear in their faces, because there is a huge hospital there. I say hospital but it is more a refuge dump where they jail all the misfits of the county, people who are different, some are crazy sure, but others are just different. There they all go and are tortured with electricity, and their families never see them again. The place is huge as well, far too big for a county such as this. Worcester is a city which lives in a shadow and the shadow is that place, everyone fears they will end up there. That's why Fitzroy shouldn't worry so much about Lenin, in this country we would simply throw him into a place like that and he would never come out again. So you see to the outside world Powick is a place where the civil war was fought, but to the people round here it is a place of terror," Donald whispered.

I nodded, "it is funny how you can drive through a place and miss it all."

"The same as people driving past this place," Donald replied.

"I bought a kettle back in London," I mused, "I'll make a fire and make some tea."

Donald lay back and looked as if I had just told him I had arranged for him a French mademoiselle to make love to, "that's one thing all we British agree with, English, Welsh and Scots, we all love tea."

I was about to go down the steps when Donald edged over to the battlements and hissed, "Simmonds!"

"What is it?"

"Is that him? Look!"

I looked at Donald before walking over to the battlements, over the brow of the hill the cyclist came, unsteady, fighting to keep a straight line, on a busy road he would be beneath a lorry. I wished that he wouldn't come, that they had left Worcestershire once they knew that I was onto them, but of course I knew that he would come, "yes that's him."

Donald looked at him and smiled, "look at him, he hasn't ridden a bike since he was a kid."

"Maybe we should call a real copper," I whispered.

"One of those country coppers?" Donald sneered, "this lot would eat him for breakfast."
"You don't even know who they are," I argued.

"You remember back in Romania how little respect we had for police," Donald replied.

"Yes," I remembered Donald beating a Romanian policeman almost to death, in fact he might have died, I remember seeing him in my rear view mirror just a crumpled mass on the ground, a mass that didn't move. The policeman's crime was just he had been in the wrong place at the wrong time and had seen things that he shouldn't have.

"When you are working for your country you don't worry about police," Donald explained. "Now when he gets near shout 'Defford!'"

I nodded and edged towards the edge, the cyclist was picking up speed now coming down the bank, it was him alright, Defford, or whatever his name was, Donald raised his hand and then hissed, "now do it!"

"Defford!" I shouted.

"What did he do?" Donald hissed.

"It's like he never heard me, he is just carrying on," I replied.

"Do it again!" Donald snapped.

"Defford!"

"Now what, now what?!" Donald fidgeted agitated.

I drew back, "this time he is looking."

Donald nodded and smiled.

"What does that prove then?" I asked.

"He forgot his alias old boy, people always do that, he only remembered it after you had shouted it again. Now get down there and invite him," Donald ordered.

I hesitated as I saw Donald glance over one of his guns again, before his eyes rose to me:

"Go on man!"

I paused again before heading down, while behind me Donald rose to his feet before following me down like Nosferatu. I felt like opening the door and running out, running as far from here I could, leaving all this craziness far behind me. I looked back and saw his eyes glinting like a Halloween pumpkin, something had changed in him, maybe Russia had changed him, God only knew what had gone on over there. I paused before the door, and looked back, "maybe I shouldn't."

"Do it man!" Donald hissed.

I sighed before opening the door, Defford and I looked at each other differently now, his eyes were bubbling with anger, but still he carried on the masquerade, less effort now was put into the Worcestershire accent, or maybe he was now overdoing it, like a serious actor who knew he was getting nowhere so now played it for laughs, "I thought I yeard something Mr Simmonds, do you need any help?"

"-Er yes Constable Defford," I replied.

He even tipped his forelock.

"I think I was followed today, I mean when I came out of here," I started.

"Do you now?" He seemed to mock.

"Yes all the way to Tenbury Wells," I added.

"Tenbury Wells," Defford mused rubbing his chin, "that's a long way, why-"

The door then opened behind me and one of Donald's pistol came out like a snake, "yes and so is bloody Moscow! 'Now come inside,' said the spider to the fly."

Defford's face flushed with panic, "now what's going on here then? I warn you don't do anything stupid because they know that I am here and they will send other constables, you can't get away with this!"

"You're no policeman," Donald snarled, "not unless you are Bolshevik police, is that who you are working for?"

The accent fell a bit, "don't be stupid man!"

"Get inside!"

"You'll hang for this!"

"They'll never find a rope long enough for me!" Donald sneered.

Gingerly Defford entered the room kept from darkness only by a single electric bulb and Donald closed the door behind us like the devil shutting the gates of hell, he then handed me the other pistol, "what are you doing?" I stammered.

"Take it man!" Donald's eyes were icy cold, "get over there and if he makes any sudden movements kill him!"

"Who do you think I am?" Defford pleaded.

"I don't know who the hell you are!" Donald replied, "but I am not going to get killed by someone I underestimated."

"I've got back up!" He spat.

"Yes of course you have, but they don't know what's going on here, and if they do they will have to be ghosts to pass through these walls, now who are you?"

"P.C Defford, Worcestershire police."

"Really," Donald looked away before his eyes rounded in fury and he looked Defford straight in the eyes before squeezing the trigger. Bang! The shot thundered out a thousand times over and the three of us staggered back deafened, through the ringing in my head I heard Defford's screams, his face seemed to melt as he staggered back with a fountain of red bursting from his leg.

"You've shot him! You've shot him!" I shouted.

Donald nodded, "so I did." He looked at the man writhing on the floor as a lion would watch a dying fawn.

"But why?"

Donald then drew back and his face became a lake of calm again, "I reckon we have half an hour before his comrades come looking for him, we don't have time for tea and scones."

"He could bleed to death from that!"

Donald nodded, "he may do if he doesn't get treated."

"Let me do something at least," I edged forwards.

"Stay where you!" Donald roared before turning on his victim, "now tell me who sent you?!"

"Go to hell! You're going to kill me anyway," he whimpered.

"Now why would I do that? If you get out of here you're not going to go to the police are you?" Donald grinned.

"Maybe he is the police!" I blurted.

"Of course he isn't the police!" Donald replied before his eyes rounded on him again, "now who are you?"

"Go to hell," Defford replied, trying to stem the blood with his hand.

"That just prolongs it," Donald laughed. "Next bullet will be to a knee cap, a knee cap wound never heals."

"You evil bastard!" Defford retorted.

Donald nodded, "now tell me who sent you," he then drew forwards and settled his gun against one of Defford's knee caps as I watched the spots of blood burn on the light bulb, "at this range I might blow your leg into two pieces, then you'll be like Humpty Dumpty, now who sent you?"

"You are right it is the Russians, I am working for the Russians!" Defford spat.

"You're a bloody liar Defford! They don't call themselves Russians anymore!"

"It's true I tell you!" Defford screamed.

I watched the blood form a pool around him, "you know I need to do something to that wound."

"Stay where you are!" Donald shrieked at me like a hysterical woman.

"But he'll die!"

"Then he'll die! Millions died in the war!"

I looked down at the gun in my hand and thought about using it on Donald.

"What's Trotsky's real name?" Donald snapped.

"What?" Defford cried.

"See! You don't even know who Trotsky is! What kind of Bolshevik are you?"

"Go to hell you limey bastard," Defford whimpered.

Donald then drew back, and looked at me, there was something different in Defford's voice that time, the yokel in his voice had gone to be replaced by an accent I had only heard in the last months of the war, he then looked at me, "he's an American.'

"But they're our friends," I replied.

Donald smiled broadly, "since when? You should read your history better Simmonds." His eyes then returned to his victim, "now how much do you know?"

Defford smiled through his suffering, "we know that the crown owns this place."

"The crown owns the whole bloody country," Donald laughed, "you don't know anything you bloody Yank!"

"We know about the baby," Defford added.

Donald's face fell, he was no actor, "what baby?"

"The baby born in London, the royal baby."

"Now can I do something?" I begged, "he's talking isn't he?"

Donald seemed in a daze for a few moments then he nodded, "alright but give me the gun first."

I gave Donald the gun and he leveled that one on Defford as well. Feverously I tried to stop the blood , yanking off my belt and tying it around his leg, I seemed as scared as he was, I could feel my hands shaking, it was funny how much of blood you saw you never seemed to get use to it. "This man is crazy, he's going to get you killed," the American moaned.

"Now tell me more my colonial cousin," Donald spoke coldly, "before I give my man another wound to treat."

"We followed you from London, we were on that train with you, we knew about this place and thought that you'd be heading here, there seemed no reason to follow you from Worcester," Defford explained.

Donald cursed himself, how didn't he notice them? He should have walked around the train instead of just sitting with Matilda, but then maybe they would have tried to snatch the baby. "You figured wrong Yank."

Defford nodded, wincing as I pulled the belt as tight as I could, "yes but we're getting warm aren't we?"

I couldn't help remember the last time that I had done this, in a fox hole with mud showering down on me, the man had died that time. Defford though was getting stronger, braver as well now he knew that he wasn't going to be killed.

"What is it to you Yank, royal babies and all that?" Donald asked.

"You have something of ours," Defford smiled.

"And what is that?"

"Canada," he replied, "every year we review our plans to invade and every year we see that the British Empire is too strong. If we invaded your dominion then you would pour men in from India and we would be knee deep in turbans before we knew what was happening."

"You wiped out one lot of Indians before I'm sure that you would manage to do it again," Donald replied.

"No what we need to do is to show our Canadian brothers that the royal family is no good, then we won't have to invade they will join us willingly," Defford smiled.

"They will never join you!" Donald warned.

"If the scandal is big enough they will," Defford's smile broadened, so much so that Donald felt like squeezing a shot into him just to wipe it off his face.

"There is no scandal here, you are barking up the wrong tree," Donald replied.

"Are we?"

Donald then drew back, he admired the defiance in Defford's eyes even though he was bleeding to death. He could understand why someone would die for a country like Britain or France but not America, a place founded only a few centuries ago, made up of immigrants from England, Ireland and who knows where else. I mean American wasn't a tribe or a language, it was nothing. "Simmonds get this man into the car, we'll dump him in the city, next to the hospital, I don't want his death on my conscience."

"So you have one then?" I quipped, "but what if we're followed?"

"Then we'll dump him by the side of the road and give his friends the choice of whether to save him or to follow us," Donald shrugged. "he's lying about one thing."

"What's that?"

"It's not about Canada, there's nothing there but polar bears, no they just want to wreck things because it's what they like to do." Donald now looked at him in contempt, he hated Americans.

As I helped Defford to his feet my eyes turned to Donald, "so did you ever meet Trotsky?"

"I never met him," Donald replied, "but I tried to kill him once."

I helped Defford out to the car, leaving Donald to look over his torture chamber before he flicked the light off and closed the door and locked it. His eyes then settled on Defford's bike, it would rust there if someone didn't steal it first.

Chapter Six: The bad Samaritans.

It was a long, silent journey back to Worcester, Defford was still bleeding but it was more a trickle now, I had saved his life! That kind of made me feel good, after all the people I had killed, I had saved at least one life. He was weak and drowsy, but I shook him to keep him awake, fearing that if he fell asleep it would be a sleep he would not wake up from."Come on man, you have to get through this, you have to get back to the States to see your family again."

"I have no family," he murmured. "Renda likes orphans."

"Renda?" I frowned.

"Must be his boss," Donald glanced back at us.

"Have you ever heard the name before?" I asked.

"Never," he replied.

Donald now drove and watched us in the back, the two revolvers sat on the passenger seat, "you did well back there Simmonds."

"What do you mean?" I frowned.

"You know the good copper, bad copper act."

"It was no act," I replied.

He nodded and smiled, then that meant I was still an idiot. We passed all the same places we had passed coming in, though now we were travelling fast, even the hairpin bend at Severn Stoke Donald took wildly on the other side of the road. He was travelling fast to try to save the American, though he would never admit to that. Kempsey we shot through as if we had stolen the car and then we swept past the old Ketch Inn before entering Worcester.

The hospital in Worcester stood opposite the jail which was a large imposing, red brick mock castle, more ridiculous than Dunstall. It stood in some way to assuage Worcester's pride after their own castle had been demolished, and the street itself was called Castle Street, one day they would demolish that castle as well and Worcester would have no more. Donald pulled up in front of the hospital before he got out and opened the door, "get out!"

"I should help him," I begged.

"No! Sit in the passenger seat, now get out Constable Defford, or else I'll drive you back into the countryside and I'll treat you in my own way."

Defford was only half awake and looked at him as if drugged, Donald shook his head, "we don't have time for this," he then grabbed Defford's shoulders before dragging him out and leaving him on the pavement, Donald then strode across, got into the driver's seat and hammered the accelerator. I looked back to see a crowd quickly gather around the half alive American and then look after us. I then glanced over to the prison, "you belong in there Donald."

"Maybe we all do, " Donald nodded putting the guns back into his pocket.

"The safety's are on aren't they?" I asked.

Donald smiled, "don't worry."

"I have never seen you like that before."

"I try not to be like it too often," Donald replied.

"You could have killed him," I murmured.

"He got off lightly, spies are meant to be shot, you know that, whether they are German, Bolshevik or from the US of A." The car turned left on the main road north to Kidderminster, "we'll go this way." Donald then leant back and took a deep breath like an actor who had just given a great performance. "I guess this bloody suit is ruined; now it will take a lot to get all this blood out." His eyes then glided onto me, he knew that he had scared me, "you know he might be right you know."

"Who?"

"The Yank," Donald replied casually, "I mean maybe the future does belong to them, you know the republicans, the anarchists, and all the scum of the world, maybe all the dukes and earls will be swept away and the world will belong to the Americans and the Bolsheviks."

"Certainly they do seem to be sharpening their knives for us," I agreed.

"The shifty unlikeable, untrustable guy you knew at school, who use to steal things and let the whole class take the blame, well that guy is taking over. Mind you it seems strange in this age when we can sit in this kind of machine and travel to places that it use to take days to get to, now it takes hours, but we still have kings and popes and all that nonsense," Donald smiled. "Look back there, did you see that statue, the largest here, and who is to? Queen Victoria! Every city has one but what did she ever do? I mean she hardly went out through most of her reign, use to go from the highlands to the Isle of Wight and miss out everywhere in between. There is no statue to Wellington or Nelson or Newton, just her."

I looked at him not knowing if this was some test, "I don't know I think it's better to have a king than not have one."

Donald nodded, "why?"

"Sorry?" I frowned.

"Why is it better to have a king than not have one?"

I shrugged, "I don't know."

Donald laughed, "exactly. You know I never met Trotsky but I met the Tsar once, it was obvious what was going to happen but the man was too weak to stop it. We told him, we told him that he was a man walking towards a cliff, but he kept walking along it. That is royalty, do you think if the Bolsheviks came here, marched up this street, do you think our King would ride his white horse out to lead the resistance? Of course not, they would get on a plane and head to Canada and leave us to Lenin and his death camps."

"Maybe so," I shrugged, "but it's nice to have someone who is outside it all I guess, you know outside politics."

"Perhaps you are right," Donald agreed, "but they have a politics all of their own, besides it's all finished now."

'What?"

"This, now that people know it is all over, there is no secrecy now, whoever they were they know too much," he replied.

"I thought you said that they were Americans," Simmonds replied.

"Maybe they were, it's hard to keep up a false accent when you are bleeding to death," he smiled. "But I think he gave away the game a little too easy."

"You call that easy?! You nearly killed him," I protested.

"I should have killed him before he told me anything," Donald smiled.

"Do you reckon he'll make it?" I asked.

"He'll need a blood transfusion, let's hope that he isn't a rare blood group, or that the yokels round here don't put sheep blood into him," Donald smiled. "One thing's for sure they will be looking for this car now, we have to get rid of it, it sticks out a mile. Drop me off at the castle and then go somewhere."

"Where?"

"I don't know anywhere, we'll have to get something less grand," he replied, but then looked disconsolate again. I had never seen him like that before, even in the days in Romania when it seemed certain that their German King would take them in on the German side. He smiled, he had been thinking of the same thing, "you know all that work we did in Romania, in not just keeping them out of the German's hands, in not just making sure they stayed out of it but actually came in on our side, all that work counted for nothing, we got no thanks, they used Romania and threw her away, and us as well." He then looked away; maybe it wasn't that he didn't think we would win, but that he didn't believe in the fight anymore."Ah it's all going to fall apart anyway."

As we drove into the outskirts we passed a line of roofless shells that builders were clambering over. "With all the people who died in the war you'd think there'd be too many houses not too few," I noted.

He smiled, as if he hadn't heard what I had said, "of course part of the problem is them."

"Who?"I frowned.

"Them, the Royals themselves, I mean they don't help, they just sit there like fat old cats who can't be bothered to catch mice anymore. Years ago they were kept on their toes, I mean you had the House of Lancaster and the House of York and they were competing for the throne, if the King didn't do his job properly an army of malcontents was formed and the King was out, but now there are no challengers and they can do as they like. They are born in London, baptized there, married there and buried there; places like this don't ever get a look in."

"But that is the capital," I replied.

"Yes but Londoners don't appreciate it, if one royal princess was married here, just one, the people would go on about it not for years but centuries, but down there you know how ungrateful they are," Donald moaned, forgetting that was where I was from. He then shrugged, "but then maybe you are right, maybe I think too much, but London isn't the country, it is just one city."

Of course I am sat here now in 1950, the radio seems to be abating with it's Al Jolson news and morning is creeping in. Well another night has passed when they never came for me I guess. God only knows what year it is when you are reading this, maybe this has been found decades from now when the house is being refurbished or demolished. If it is the year 2000 I am sure that Britain has long since gotten rid of them. I will have to hide it well because the CIA will pick over this place with a fine tooth comb when I leave it. Sitting in 1950 Donald seems like a real visionary, because there are only two super powers now America and Russia, the Bolsheviks have rolled their border beyond Berlin, and the Americans are pulling strings on the rest of the world. They haven't invaded Canada but then they don't really need to anymore. My past seems crazy now because for over twenty years I have done very little of interest. To watch a man get tortured and then to sit next to the torturer and converse about world politics seems like something out of a strange dream.

We were well outside Worcester when we passed over the narrow river Salwarpe, the Droitwich canal ran next to it. Once the canal had been the splendorous one, alive with boats coming in and out of the town, and the river had been it's despised neighbor. The canal's days though were long past and now it was the river's turn to laugh as slowly it's artificial rival was lost beneath reeds falling into disrepair, no boat had passed up it for years.

After a long silence Donald sighed, "I'll tell you what drive back to the castle; we will decide what to do there. Oh and don't say anything to Fitzroy about our discussions about monarchy."

"Why?" I asked.

"Well you know he wouldn't understand, " Donald replied.

"He doesn't share your republican views," I argued.

"No his problems lie in a different area," Donald hinted.

"What do you mean?"
Donald though ignored me.

The castle couldn't be seen from the high ground coming out of Ombersley and couldn't be seen from the river as we passed over the Thomas Telford Bridge at Holt Fleet, Matilda only glimpsed the Severn through branches that masked the castle, to the outside world the place had never existed. Yet the Americans were on the brink of finding it like some lost Amazonian temple and violating it's secret.

"I am just wondering if any of this is my fault," Donald moaned as we passed over the river. "I mean how did they find out, who told them?"

I shrugged, "maybe it was Fitzroy."

"No it couldn't be, he wouldn't know who to phone," Donald replied.

"Maybe his sons said something when they went off to war," I mused.

Donald nodded, "yes that's more likely, but it sure has taken the Americans long enough to find us."

Matilda was watching from the window as the car pulled in, she had been in the room most of the day but had heard Mrs Fitzroy outside spying on her; the floor boards were too creaky for her to rest her feet on them silently. She had kept the door locked as well. I knew she was watching me, she had heard the gate scrape open and had gone to the other side of the house with the baby, and she never left her side now. She noticed as I got out that I never bothered to open Donald's door, she told me that that day I had had more of a swagger, looking more the soldier of 1918 than 1914, who had seen it all and no longer cared about anything. She then watched Fitzroy hurry over and start talking to Donald before he ushered him away, Donald nodded back to me and then raised his finger to his lips. That was all Matilda needed to know that I could be trusted. Fitzroy and Donald entered the house and Matilda tip toed as silently as she could, edging out onto the landing and peering down the steps, drawing closer and closer to Fitzroy's broad Worcestershire accent:

"I tell you this is trouble, I can smell it."

"Oh I don't know, they didn't know much, they were clutching at straws really," Donald lied.

"You should have killed him," Fitzroy replied.

"That wouldn't have solved anything," Donald snapped.

"At least that would have been one less person who knew, they were Americans you said," he grunted.

"Yes," Donald's face twitched with irritation.

"They probably want Jamaica off us," Fitzroy cackled.

"They said Canada," Donald replied.

"Oh they want that as well do they? Greedy bastards, they already took New York off us, what more do they want? We paid for New York; we paid the Dutch for it!" Fitzroy moaned.

"I'd like to know how they found out," Donald replied.

"They must have read that French book," he retorted.

"What French book?" Donald frowned.

"That book that Alexander Dunmass wrote," Fitzroy replied.

"Alexander Dunmass?" Donald frowned, "you mean Alexander Dumas."

"Whatever, when it came out it sent the family into a panic, they thought he was writing about them not King Louis of France, they couldn't figure how he knew so much. The world has changed now anyway, I knew that we were going to have problems, there are news reels now, I see one the last time I went to St John's, there is a cinema there you know, then of course there are newspapers as well. Everyone knows, even here in Caerwrangon, everyone knows what the King's children look like."

Matilda drew back and looked down at the baby, was this the King's child? But how was that possible?

"I will send Simmonds into the city later, is there anything you want?" Donald changed the subject.

Fitzroy though continued, "then think about what happens when the nipper grows up."

Donald paused, "you can have surgery these days to change someone's face, and they could even make you handsome Fitzroy."

Fitzroy ignored the taunt and showed a sharpness of mind which belied his station in life, but then stuck here in Holt what else had he had to think about all these years?"What of the surgeon? What of the nurses? They will have seen the face before we change it."

"Then we will kill them," Donald replied as if it was the simplest thing in the world.

Matilda imagined Fitzroy's jaw dropping but it never instead he rounded on Donald like a terrier, "more bodies, more loose ends, and more investigations. Better kill the baby."

Matilda stepped back and pulled the baby close to her and prayed that she never cried but she stepped back and a floorboard betrayed her. Donald's eyes shot up instantly and he stepped forwards.

"Do you think that she heard us?" Fitzroy hissed.

"Better to take for granted that she did," Donald replied.

"What are you going to do with her? Kill her too?" Fitzroy whispered.

Slowly Matilda walked down the stairs, trying to act like there was nothing wrong; that she had heard nothing, a smile forced it's way up on her face as if it was made of stone. Four eyes met hers, desperate eyes like those of wolves. Tightly she pulled the baby close to her, and she closed her eyes and whispered a prayer to God that the baby would be safe.

Donald's smile was as false as Matilda's, "how's the baby?"

"She's asleep," Matilda replied.

"Good," he nodded.

Matilda walked past them and outside. Donald's eyes streaked after her, "she heard us."

Matilda had to talk to the chauffeur, I was sponging at the blood as she walked over and I jolted as she called, "Simmonds."

I turned and breathed a sigh of relief when I saw it was her, "please call me Charlie."

"What's happened?" She asked.

"Someone was bleeding in the car," I replied.

"Why?"

"Because Donald shot him," I answered.

She gasped, but wasn't as shocked as she should have been, "what happened?"

"Someone was watching the place where Donald sent me, and he wanted to know why."

"So he shot him?!"
I shrugged, "he said it would make him talk more quickly, and it worked he talked alright, afterwards we drove him to a hospital in Worcester or Caerwrangon or whatever they are calling it today."

"He shot someone," Matilda repeated as if expecting me to say no it was a joke.

I nodded, "yes and he was ready to kill him too, he shot him and felt nothing as he was bleeding to death, he just watched him like a cat."

She gazed back to where she knew they were watching, before leaning forwards in a whisper, "you know him, I mean you were with him in the war, would he kill us do you think?"

I nodded, "he is capable of anything, he always was I guess but now he is crazy. I have never seen a face like that since the war then it was a German coming at me with a bayonet. If he had to he would kill you and me."

"How about the baby?"

I nodded, "no problem for him."

Her eyes then probed my face, "but he is a friend of yours from the war isn't he?"

She didn't trust me, but then trust is a hard thing to come by, "no, I doubt that he has any friends."

"But you speak Romanian together," she argued.

"Because we were both there, but we were not friends, he gave the orders and I followed them, like now," I looked her straight in the eyes so that she knew that she could trust me, "he cares nothing for me, I am nothing to him."

"So who was the man he shot?" She asked.

"An American spy, so he said, maybe he was, maybe he wasn't," I shrugged.

"America?! What has it got to do with them?" She asked.

"Apparently they have a plan to invade Canada and they plan to start here in Worcestershire," I smiled but it was a smile full of sadness.

She glanced back at the castle again, I wish she would stop doing that because that told them that we were speaking about them, "have you ever heard of a French writer called Alexander Dumas?"

I laughed, "I have trouble reading English let alone French."

"They are sending you into Worcester later, see if you can buy his books."

"Anyone in particular?" I asked.

"I don't know get all of them," she replied, "because one of them is about us, I mean about what all this is about."

"Alexander Dumas," I repeated.

"Yes," she nodded.

"I'll remember that."

She then drew forwards, "one thing Charlie, I think we need to get out of here."

I heard the door and so leant forwards, stroking my hand down her arm and bending down as if about to kiss her, before turning towards the two eyes which I knew were watching me. Donald looked like a giant crow as he strode over to us, "Simmonds I wonder if you could go into Virgornia for me."

My eyes fell on her, she was a little shocked at my romantic advance, "look after yourself and the baby, I will get us out of this, I've gotten out of worse places." I even winked at her.

I then walked over to Donald whose face was as stern as a school master's, "what did she want?"

"Oh her, she was worried about the baby and because I told her I was a father she came to me," I lied. I am a better liar than Matilda or Donald but he didn't believe a word of it, whatever we were going to do we had to do it quickly.

He then produced his list, "here these are the things that I want you to get."

I read down it, I could add Alexander Dumas novels to the bottom of it, "no problem."

I was about to head over to the car when his hand settled on my shoulder, "did you tell her what happened today?"

"I didn't tell her all, but I had to say something, she saw me sponging the blood out," I replied.

Donald nodded, he accepted that.

As I got into the car and Fitzroy hurried out to open the gate Donald's eyes settled on Matilda, there was no way she could hide the fear in her face. I started the car up and my eyes were fixed in the rear view mirror as I drove off. What a fine Sir Galahad I am, worrying about a woman and a baby who were nothing to me when I have my own wife and son in London I had just walked out on.

Donald glanced towards the car as it pulled off, before pulling out a large, old key, "what is that?"

"The key to the church," he smiled, "would you like to look inside?"

"I don't know," she shrugged.

"It is a special one, going back to the Normans," he then strode forwards and opened the lychgate. He then began to act like a tour guide, "that large stone down there was for people to mount their horses and dismount. The tower is 14th century, that side of the church is from 1660 and that 1789. Look at that, that is Norman, you see how it is rounded in the Norman style."

Matilda nodded, she could see that he was trying to reach out to her, but it was no use they were just too different. Matilda went to church to try to feel God, to reach out to Him, Donald went more to see history. He seemed to relish the word Normans as if they had been magic beings from another world. Besides of course Matilda knew that he had nearly killed someone today and had talked of infanticide, the most horrible word in the English language, he should be coming to church to make his peace not look at it's architecture. Gingerly she walked under the lychgate, she noticed that the graveyard had been cleared and all the tombstones seemed to have been all barged out to the walls, these were the ancestors of the people at Holt Heath and their graves were visited no more, so the stones were in a purgatory between being honoured and being smashed up. Donald looked back before jamming the key into the lock and pushing it open and letting all the musk of centuries escape. He then beckoned her forwards, and lightly lifted up a lantern that had been left by the door, he checked it, it must have been Fitzroy's for when he came in here. Donald lit it and the light danced off the coloured glass of one of the windows, "that window is," he started and then fell silent as saw Matilda was captivated. She stepped forwards, whatever you think of the church, of religion, of God there is always something magic in these places, the residue of untold centuries of prayer, going back to the beginnings of Christianity and beyond into paganism. For Donald religion was only for people with small libraries, he watched Matilda like a primitive African girl faced by a statue of her tribal god. At the far side the light danced off the gold of a mosaic, which was as out of place here as a zebra on the Russian steppe, one of the previous Lords had brought that back from Italy and planted it here in Normanesque England.

Matilda drifted into the chapel which ran parallel to the nave, stepping inside her eyes rested on where a stone woman lay, "who was that?"

Donald smiled, "the lover of good King John, he loved her to the grave, so they say, but she could never become his Queen."

Matilda looked at him, "why?"

"He was a King, of royal blood, she was a great beauty, the most beautiful woman in the land, but that beauty counted for nothing because she was just a peasant girl. It is for the poor to fall in love, the royals cannot do that." Donald smiled, "thank God I am not one of them, when I marry I will marry for love."

Matilda looked at him, then the baby whimpered and her eyes sank to her, of course she could never have anything to do with a man who could even think of killing a baby, "I'd better get her inside."

Donald cursed and his eyes settled on her bottom as she walked out, before turning to face the blessed Virgin, what kind of a man was he to have pornographic thoughts in a church? The door closed behind her and he cursed, he was no good at this, maybe it was his height that always spoilt it for him, maybe they saw him as a freak, but if he couldn't even get a servant girl, a girl from Cheapside then it was a pretty poor state of affairs. He then looked back over the church; one thing was for sure he had to get me out of the way, back to London or dead.

I parked the car in St John's and then walked past the cricket ground down towards the city, past the gate of cripples, some still wearing their uniforms from the war. I felt some shame walking past them and thought about the time I had held back in a foxhole, I was about to go when a Tommy had passed me, then I watched as he lurched back with a bullet in his head, and I scrambled out of the way of his corpse as if it was a falling tree. Maybe that was the difference between me and them; maybe they had been braver than I had. I could almost hear their thoughts, I was another man who had dodged the war and come back intact, if they said anything what could I say? That I had just been lucky and God had cursed them, why? I didn't even know the name of the man who had taken my bullet. I couldn't look at them, the conquerors of the German, Austrian and Turkish Empires, I hurried past them into the park which lay behind.

Worcester hardly looked like a city at the heart of the greatest empire on earth; money is like a river which always runs in a different direction to you. The poorest lived next to the Severn, in flood hovels, it wasn't just the soldiers who had been conned, we all had. However poor must life in the country be for them to come and live in that squalor instead of going back there? I looked over to the prison and it's mock gothic battlements, I thought about Defford, maybe I should visit him, but that might be dangerous, but then how dangerous could a man with one good leg be? As I walked out of the park I pulled out Donald's list and looked at the first thing written, to go to the post office and pick up his messages, whatever that meant, maybe it was the orders from his boss, Donald wouldn't do anything without those orders, if he never got them then he was like a car waiting for the key to be turned. There were various food stuffs, I smiled including Worcester source, and then I would track down Matilda's French writer.

The city was filled with the kind of folk that you never saw in London, raw country yokels spattered with mud and animal blood, mixing with them were the factory workers. Even in Worcester there were factories, making the source of course, but also gloves and china , that were to be exported all over the world. I tracked down a very small book shop in a back alley. Second hand book shops I guess are a bit like old churches, there is the same musk, but in there it is the smell of old paper, and instead of centuries of prayers you have years, sometimes centuries of studying. Of course I had heard of Dumas but I didn't want Matilda to think that I was too clever in case she thought that I was too much like Donald. I emerged with 'the Three Musketeers' and 'the Man in the Iron Mask.' I looked at the first book, I wonder who that was about, me, Donald and Fitzroy maybe, I smiled. I tried to flick through it, but of course it was impossible on a crowded pavement.

I then headed for the hospital past a boarded up shop where a Tsarist style pogrom had taken place right here in sleepy Worcester. A German had once lived there, he had come from his homeland with a talent for mending clocks and watches and he built up a business here, where he was seen as nothing short of a magician, for he knew things unknown of outside of the Fatherland. He had been slowly becoming rich and furnished the wall outside his shop with great clock dials, then the war came, and then it had fallen apart. The whole city knew he was a German, he had never hidden the fact, he wasn't Dutch or Swiss he was German, the night war broke out a gang of all the scum of the city had smashed into his shop and threw him out on the street. I remember myself in those days in London and I felt ashamed, because I had been as infected as anyone, the rape of Belgium! Babies impaled on spikes! Nuns raped! If I had been in Worcester I would have been part of that gang, if we wanted to attack a German there was one in Buckingham Palace and he was a lot guiltier than this clock mender.

I passed under the railway bridge and I looked over to where I had parked that day and waited for Donald, it seemed a lifetime ago now. I had been happy to get a well paid job, to get out of London, to get away from my wife. Now I wish I could turn the clock back, but then I knew now and if I had known I would have still have still come here, for the baby.

The hospital of course was another great Victorian building, I entered and asked for Defford, at first they looked at me strangely, until I mentioned the gunshot wound, then I was shown straight into the ward where he lay, looking more angry than sick. I paused for a moment as the nurse left, not knowing whether to go again but then he had seen me and it was too late and he crawled back up the headboard, as if Donald had changed his mind and sent me to kill him. I nodded and then edged forwards; somehow he looked more American now, like the soldiers I had seen enter the trenches in the last days. They had looked more like actors going into one of their films, with their crisp uniforms and fresh faces, those uniforms had stayed crisp until the final shot. They had contrasted sharply next to us, a group of ragged warriors, their uniforms had been more stylish than ours even before ours had been dragged through the mud and washed in blood. They had stayed smart until 1919 when they had strode into the Versailles peace talks as if they had been there from the start and had suffered as much as the rest of us, the Romanians had not even been allowed into the room,.

"How are you doing?" I nodded.

Defford turned and looked at me in disbelief, "is this some kind of joke?"

"Hey you know I wasn't in favour of all that," I pointed down at his leg now in plaster, proof that it all been no nightmare. "How is your leg?"

"I was lucky apparently," he grunted and looked away, "never broke any bones."

I nodded, "you were lucky normally a bullet makes a lot of mess when goes in."

"Of course you'd know more about that than I would," he replied bitterly.

I drew back, "you should be careful you are playing with the big boys now."

"What are you here for?" he spat.

"Just to make sure that you are alright," I replied.

"Really," Defford scowled.

"So are you really American?"

"What of it?"

"It's just that your accent was very good," I nodded.

"Obviously not good enough, "Defford looked away. Then he looked back, "why don't you come and work for us. It was a man from here who helped me with the accent. We have a lot of limeys, -er British working for us, you'd be surprised."

"Now why would I do that?"

Now Defford smiled, and there was mockery in it, "might as well be on the winning side, these great European empires will fall like dominoes, the future is American, we've wiped all our natives out, they can't rise up against us but yours will."

I shrugged, "maybe, maybe not."

Defford leant forwards, "then tell me why you are here? You don't give a damned about me, how many men did you see wounded during the war? Did you track them all down?"

"Of course not."

"So why are you here?" Defford smile widened.

I put my shopping down allowing Defford's eyes to settle on it, reading the titles of the books, his eyes narrowed.

"I don't trust the man who shot you," I started.

"Who Donald Pembridge?" Defford replied and watched my reaction, "oh yes we know who he is. You are wise not to trust him, you saw how quickly he shot me, don't doubt that he would kill you if you get in his way."

"Yes well I don't trust you either," I replied.

Defford laughed, "you're wise on that one as well."

"I mean I don't even know you're real name, it's not Defford, I know that."

He smiled, "that was the first thing that came into my head that day. I had passed through the place while trying to learn to ride that bloody bike, you can keep the bike if you like, a present from your Uncle Sam, I don't ever want to see it again."

I nodded, "thanks."

"How well do you know him then?"

"He was my CO in the war; we faced death together many times."

"Your CO hey? The kindly officer who was like a father to his men," Defford laughed.

"Not exactly," I confessed.

"So what do you plan to do Charlie?"

"I haven't decided that yet, if I do decide I need your help what do I do?"

Defford nodded and he gave a gritted teeth smile, as if his team had just won a match, "not here, I do not know how long I will be here."

"So where then?"

"My boss is a man called Renda, he is staying at the Star Hotel, you know the one by-"

I interrupted him with a smile, "yes I know the place. That's where the great and good of Worcester society go if you can call it that."

Defford chuckled, "yes they all smell of pig swill and piss around here."

"I suppose he doesn't have a first name," I asked.

"That's right, he doesn't," Defford replied.

"Well I guess he'll be the only one staying there with that name anyway," I mused.

"Yes that's right, there ain't many foreigners around here, they probably ate the last lot who came here. You know he was pretty pissed off that day in Tenbury Wells."

"You were there?" I asked.

He nodded, "yes , I thought it was funny in a way, imagine us falling for an old trick like that. We were hours as well there, because we never had a spare. Hours are like days in a place like that."

"How are you going to take over the world without a spare tyre?" I mocked. "So what is all this about, I mean with the baby?"

"Is the baby dark?"

"No, how do you mean?"

"The royal family has a colour bar. That is why they marry people they hate like the Russians, Bulgarians and Germans but they can't marry into families they like, like the Japanese and the Thais," Defford told me.

"Maybe the Thais and Japanese wouldn't have them," I retorted.

Defford smiled, "yes maybe."

"The child is white," I stated.

Defford nodded, "then it is not that, and it can't be that the child is illegitimate."

"Why not?"

"That has never bothered them in the past; they have always had the morality of farm animals, why should it bother them now?" Defford grinned.

My eyes sank, I was no royalist, I was always a realist, but there is something as an Englishman hearing the royals slated by a man with an American accent which rankled in me, maybe I was still their serf at heart.

"No there must be something about this child which marks him out as different," he asked.

"Her," I corrected.

"Her?" He looked up.

Simmonds nodded.

"Then it is a girl?"

"Yes, why does that change anything?"

Defford's lip bulged out and he shrugged, "no not really, how about Down's Syndrome?"

"What's that?" I asked.

Defford smiled, "something that no heir to the throne can have, you would see it in the face if she has it."

"No I've not noticed anything. So what do you plan to do with the child?" I edged forwards, "kill her?"

"Good Lord no, it's your friend Donald who will do that!" The American replied, "if the child is an embarrassment to the family they will kill it, just like a gull throwing the littlest chick out of the nest. They do not think like us Charlie, they have not gone to the same schools we have, and they haven't worked in the same places, walked down the same streets. They've never been broke, never wondered where the next meal was coming from. Not just them but their fathers and grandfathers and their fathers and their grandfathers never had that worry."

I smiled, "and don't tell me you people are different."

Defford smiled broadly, "maybe not, but if the baby was with us she would never come to harm, because she is our ace, we can use her to play it against the British, well for as long as you keep your silly kings and queens anyway."

I drew back, "so you're asking me to betray my own country, the country I faced certain death to defend."

Defford now openly mocked, "yes and where did it get you? Some people came out of that war looking mighty pretty, the same people who always do."

I looked at him, "yes you people for one."

Defford ignored that, "I know this is a big step, but think of how you will feel like if they kill the baby."

He was right, but was a baby worth as much as a whole empire? But if the empire was rotten, if it killed babies then it deserved to come crashing down, "I won't feel too good if I betray my country."

Defford looked at me and came out with one of those arguments he had learnt stateside, "what language do you speak?"

"English of course," I replied.

"What race are you?"

"English," I replied.

Defford then smiled, "then what is your country?"

"England," I replied then paused.

Defford then smiled broadly, "no it isn't."

I looked at him, I knew what he meant, "well I'm glad that you are looking better." I drew back then like a normal visitor who had visited a normal patient.

"Are you going then?"

I nodded, "yes that was the general idea, and I'm not hanging around for your pals to show up."

Defford grinned, "that's maybe wise they are not as placid as I am."

"When you get back to America give my best to Charlie Chaplin tell me we all miss him."

Chapter Seven:`A Bolshevik soul.

Kondrakov was waiting outside the hospital, leant against the prison wall, pretending to read the Berrows's journal, the world's oldest newspaper, or so it said. It was amazing how it could keep running in a city where nothing ever happened. Behind him arms hung out from the bars, as inmates pressed themselves against them, like plants trying to get as close to the sunlight as they could. Kondrakov looked back at them, they were broken men, too dispirited even to hurl abuse at him, like zoo animals. one old man though moaned, "get word to my wife will you Sir?"

Kondrakov looked back with a cruel smile, "she's probably sleeping with half the city now, I doubt she'll have time for me."

"Why you fucking bastard," he cursed.

Suddenly Kondrakov threw the journal over the wall as he watched me emerge, I noticed that, and through the corner of my eye I saw him walk across the road towards me. He was barely twenty and had a face that seldom smiled; he had to feed his lunges with a constant stream of cigarette smoke. He looked foreign, it was hard to put my finger on, he was blond haired and brown eyed, maybe it was the fact that he had high cheek bones, he didn't seem to blend in with the figures around him, his clothes were different, not vastly different but they were clothes that the English shops never sold. He spoke English, Russian and Estonian all without an accent, but he was only a shadow of a man because he felt nothing, no love, no lust, nothing. Maybe it's because I had been followed in Bucharest many times and I knew the routine, I was on my guard for men loitering and the walking as soon as I appeared, like one of those figures on a clock waiting for the hour to sound.

I headed over the road, I didn't look back once, I didn't have to, I made my way into town, there were alleyways I could have darted down but I judged it better not to, firstly he was younger than me and secondly I was carrying shopping. I could have just waited in the alley and grabbed him, but maybe he had a gun and secondly maybe he was tougher than he looked, a boxer or something. As I passed the passageways I knew that it made him feel more secure made him feel that I didn't know he was behind me, because I hadn't grabbed a chance of escape. I looked at one of the novels again, and flicked through the pages, before I nearly walked into some old woman. Kondrakov juddered to a halt behind me as I stopped to apologize, I glanced back slightly, he was on the floor doing up the laces he had undone, hoping that I wouldn't start talking to the woman. I smiled and headed away quickly; Kondrakov got up and followed me with his shoe untied.

"Hey your shoe's untied," a passer by pointed to his foot.

"Fuck off!" Kondrakov snarled and the man staggered back astounded.

I then stopped at a main road, I looked at the sign 'Town Ditch' then I watched a bus coming down the road towards me, it was not going to stop but was going to have to slow down right in front of me. I looked back at my pursuer and then the bus. Then I looked back again and this time I looked Kondrakov right in the eye and smiled, a shot of panic raced through his face, as the bus slowed before me I leapt onto it shopping bags and all, landing on my knees before the conductor, who sprawled back, almost into the arms of a fat old spinster, "are you a mad man?"

"No, I really need to catch this bus!" I exclaimed.

I then looked back, the bus pulled off and Kondrakov broke into a sprint and I got ready to kick him off the bus but he never made it, he tried racing it down the road and all the passengers watched him perplexed before he stopped gasping, holding his sides. I then turned round to the conductor again, "seems like a popular bus, or he's training for the Olympics, where's it going?"

"St John's," the conductor replied pulling himself up from his blushing passenger.

I laughed; I had even caught the right bus! "Drop me off at the church will you, I need to say thanks to the Lord."

Kondrakov was still down the street bent double coughing, these young guys just didn't have it, and he wouldn't have lasted a day in Flanders. Cutting out the cigarettes would help of course, I had been offered some in the trenches and had told them he would rather have the Kaiser's quick death than Woodbine's slow one. When it came to running for my life I wanted my lunges to be working and cigarettes robbed your breath.

Kondrakov cursed before rising up again and heading back to the hospital, he didn't fancy facing Renda after he had stood in front of the hospital for twenty minutes then to follow someone only to lose them. He had underestimated me, that was part of his problem and in fact he knew it, he always thought he was cleverer than he was and the world around him was made up of lesser beings. I guess they weren't to know about my time in Romania and must have thought I was just another down on his luck ex-soldier. Kondrakov was afraid of his boss, he told himself that he wasn't, but he was. He was a Russian who had come out of the civil war; he had seen bodies in the streets and women raped in front of him. Renda was from the easy life of Middle America, he had lived off the fat of the land, and yet he was afraid of him. Kondrakov finished off one cigarette and quickly lit another, sucking in it's poison like an asthmatic on an inhaler, he was preparing his story over and over again in his head. A great red brick railway viaduct ran out over the city from Foregate Street station to the river, he headed under it's arches, maybe he would tell him that I had pulled a gun. Yes, that was it! Whatever story he came out with though it didn't sound good. He decided to go to the hospital first, talk to Defford, yes he would put off seeing Renda until later, much later, he'd have a drink first. When he got to the ward though Renda was there and glared at him, "you lost him didn't you?"

Kondrakov was amazed, it was as if Renda had a third eye or something, he nodded.

"You bastard!" Renda slowly rose to his feet, "you stupid Russian bastard" Anger stoked in his eyes, a burning fury that you could run power stations off. He then looked over to the matron and remembered where he was and smiled in embarrassment, "sorry mam." Renda then nodded, "he's a clever one that one."

"I didn't think that he saw me he never looked back once, and then suddenly just jumped onto a bus."

Renda smiled, "not bad for a chauffeur, maybe I should shoot you and give him your job." It was no idle threat, he reminded Kondrakov of a devil, with is black and beard coming to a point on his chin, it was graying now. He was getting old but he was still young in his mind. "You know Kondrakov, I didn't come off some stinking refugee boat across the Bearing Straits."

"There were Princesses and Counts on that ship," Kondrakov bleated.

"Bullshit all of it, a Prince with no money is worse than a beggar without any. I am a real Prince, a real King. I am from New Mexico, and in my town I can have any woman I want, _any_ woman! I have two things you see: One is white skin, the other is money. The women there are all brown and beautiful and whatever marriage certificates they have I own them all. One escaped once, one native girl went north, she met a white, New Hampshire dick there, a proper corn fed, apple pie eating, all American dick. Of course he had never seen a pretty Latina before and fell for her like an anvil out of a skyscraper's window; they got married and came back to my town. She thought that because her husband was white it would make her safe, she thought that she had escaped me. She tried to get me to talk to the dick but of course I never spoke to him, I turned my face away from him. I could see that she was panicking. I was the one who ignored him, but she told her husband that he was the rude one! Then I told her that he was arrogant, that he walked around like he had a king in his belly, my wife told her than he was a jealous man and worse than a Mexican."

"Your wife?" Kondrakov frowned.

"Yes, she is a lovely woman, as sick and as twisted as I am, often when I was with those women she will get into the bed with us," Renda roared.

Defford's jaw dropped but Kondrakov was enticed by the story; there was something about perversity which fascinated him.

"She is one of them, well half; her father was a white man. She has the face and body of one of them _mulattas_ you pay for down in Mobile. She told me she had had her eye on this little Mexicana for a long time and had long dreamt of having her, so she was behind me all the way! Well anyway the dick's woman came to me to apologize, apologize to me! She knew it was my entire fault, but she blamed her husband, she told him off, she stopped talking to him, she made him take off his wedding ring! Then she came and begged my forgiveness and I had her, I pulled down her dress, pulled down her panties and I had her there and then in my office. She could go back to her husband then, of course he left her eventually and she got pregnant with my child. She was a pretty little thing but I had never much cared for her, but when she showed up in my town, in my town with a white husband she occupied all my thoughts. That town is like a field of brown cows and I am the white bull, I will let a brown bull enter the town but when a white bull showed his face he had to be chased off. I do not know if it was imagination but after he left and I took her to my bed again it was the sweetest sex I ever made to any woman. I won in the end, money won."

"Aren't you afraid that your herd will scatter when you are over here," Kondrakov teased.

"I am not one bit afraid, my herd will not scatter because they are afraid of me even here. The world is not big enough for them not to be afraid of me,"Renda warned, "when I go back it will all be the same,"

"What if the husband comes back?" Kondrakov smiled.

"Then I'll kill him this time!" Renda snarled, "I'll kill him and bury him in the middle of the town, I'll even pay for the headstone, and I'll say what to write on it as well. He'll never leave New Mexico, and it is a long, long way from New Hampshire."

"If you are a rich man then why are you here?" Defford cut in.

"Do you think a man like me would ever be content with a little town in New Mexico? I want to walk down the street in New York or Los Angeles and be able to take any woman there too, but brown women are the best, coffee brown."

"Why?"

"Because when you take one you are their master!" Renda's dark eyes glinted.

Kondrakov just looked at him, he didn't like him, he wasn't use to this kind of person, Russians tended to keep their mouths shut, especially about their inner most thoughts. "But if it's power you want why aren't you in Washington? Why are you in this English backwater?"

Renda then looked at him like a camel about to attack a rival, "because this is where we will a score a greater victory over our oldest enemy, greater than any Washington achieved and I will be the man who did it." He then drew back and gave a contented smile, "quiet backwaters like this Kondrakov are the places where fathers are raping their daughters and the village priest is molesting all the boys. Something is going on here, something big. Now we can't afford to screw up, Howard here has already taken a bullet for the team; you've come away without a scratch on you! That's not good enough!" He then looked at Defford, "what did this Charlie Simmonds say?"

Defford tried to make our conversation sound better than what it was, "he is definitely thinking of joining us, and he is no baby killer. I don't know what he did in the war but he can't kill children."

Renda nodded, "a weakness we can exploit."

"He bought something in Worcester," Kondrakov added, "he had two bags with him."

Renda looked at him, "two shopping bags and he still managed to outrun you, what was in the bags? Balloons?"

Kondrakov shrugged, "the usual stuff you know."

"No I don't know Kondrakov tell me!"

"Well food things, nothing special, oh he had a book, he was looking at it," Kondrakov muttered.

"Books? Did you see what it was?" Renda leant forwards.

"No, I-"

Defford cut in, "it was someone called Alexander Dumas."

"Who the hell is that?" Renda roared.

"A French writer," Kondrakov tried to save himself, "he wrote novels."

"Novels, ah what use are they?" Renda scoffed, "I only ever use novels to light fires with. I wanted to know if they were fact books, maybe guides to some other place in England, something that will tell us where they are going to run to, if they do run. What did this Dumas write?"

"'The Corsican Brothers,'" Kondrakov replied.

"I've never read a novel in my life!" Renda boasted.

"And 'the Man in the Iron Mask!'" Kondrakov exclaimed.

Renda looked round at him, "so what?"

"Don't you see that might be our story?" Kondrakov snapped.

"See it, I've never even heard of it," Renda replied. "So what's it about?"

"It is the story of a prince who is taken at birth and imprisoned, and made to wear an iron mask, so no one can see his face," Kondrakov replied.

"Only the fucking French would think of something like that," Renda scoffed and then caught the matron's stern eye, "sorry Mam."

"So you're saying this baby is like this prince in the iron mask?" Defford cut in.

"Maybe," Kondrakov replied.

"What problem did they have with people seeing his face?" Renda asked.

"He looked exactly like the King of France, he was his exact double!" Kondrakov exclaimed.

I drove back smiling, I had outsmarted them twice now, and maybe I should make this my job. But then Germans would never have fallen for that, with a German following you, you knew you had someone who was at least as clever as you were, someone who had thought of everything. These future masters of the world made schoolboy errors, their army had been the same, making all the mistakes we had made in 1914 when they had finally arrived in 1918, there had been no telling them either. Still there was something unnerving about Kondrakov, a vacancy in his eyes as if he was only half alive. I drove north with those eyes still staring at me, maybe I had seen the man who would one day kill me. It was not a long journey, I wanted to make it longer, just carry on driving as if it was one of those roads in Russia which went on forever. I had never seen eyes like those before, a soldier's eyes are as alive as a tiger's, his were dead. I knew then that he wasn't an American; America can't produce eyes like that.

Defford was right, how would I feel if I let a baby die? A baby is defenseless in this world, and sinless as well unlike the rest of us. There was logic behind what Defford had said; of course the Yanks would keep her safe. The British Empire couldn't stand on the bones of a baby; we British were a honourable people. I drove past the mud track which lead to the castle and headed down to the river again and then parked in front of the huge pub. I looked back up towards the castle , I needed some more answers before I went back there. The pub was certainly too large for Holt Fleet and relied a lot on the boats which moored there, waiting to get through the locks, because every boat had to stop there. At Holt the river divided around an island, with the locks on one side and a weir on the other where the water thundered down day and night. That was the background noise which never left Holt Fleet. The boats were less now but still any boat which had negotiated its way through the maze of canals in Birmingham had to pass here to get downstream. I sighed before I got out of the car and walked inside, it was near empty, being near the middle of the day.

The landlord was stood behind the bar and looked at me without the usual country landlord look; he was use to outsiders coming in here and could have been working in London, "hello Sir, what will you have?"

"Hello," I smiled, "a pint please."

"Cider or beer?"

"Beer please, I'm a Londoner, I can't even spell cider, when do we ever see apples?"

The landlord grinned, "I thought you were a beer type of gentleman, when you first came through that door I thought: 'yes that's a man who likes his beer.' They are mainly cider drinkers around here you know, the further west you go the more they love their cider."

I smiled, "sorry to give myself away."

"Oh no, no, no Sir, Londoners stand out because they are more stylish and sofia- cated than us simple people from around here."

I looked around the pub, it didn't look like any simple tavern to me

"So what brings you to Holt Fleet?" The landlord asked, pouring out the beer from one of those strange pub taps, tilting the glass so that it wasn't all froth.

"Oh I have a job up here," I replied.

"Really Sir, you don't look like the farming type."

"No I am not," I smiled, "I am working up at the castle."

The landlord stopped and looked at me, "are you serious?" He settled the glass down before walking over to the window and looking out onto the car, people had told him that they had seen such a car driving around here but he had not believed them, not here.

I nodded, "sure why?"

The landlord drew back, "maybe you don't know, being from the big city and all that but you must have noticed something odd up there."

I smiled, "well they do have their own ways."

"I have lived here all my life and I have never been there, never been inside that church. That is our church, but to go to evensong we have to go up the steep bank to Ombersley, or down the river to Grimley," he moaned.

"Really?"

The landlord looked at me and paused, trying to decide if he should say any more, but in the end he couldn't resist it, "yes the couple who live there venture out now and again, but don't talk to anyone around here. Folk say that they are brother and sister."

"They certainly look like it," I agreed receiving the pint that was eventually offered to me.

"All I knows is that the folk around here want their church back, our ancestors are buried up there!" He declared, "although my father came here from Bristol and my mother was from Kidderminster," he admitted.

"Well I'm sorry about that," I smiled, "but I really don't know much about it, I've just got here."

"So who is living up there now?"

"A man and a woman and a baby." I replied.

"What a young family?" the landlord was getting more and more interested.

"No they are not married and the child is not theirs," I knew I was talking too much, but I also knew I had little time and needed answers fast; at least I wasn't shooting anyone in the leg.

The landlord frowned, "I yeard talk, I yeard talk that the castle has long been used to raise children, children that rich folks are ashamed of."

"Has anyone ever seen these children?" I asked.

The landlord shook his head, "no."

"Do they live to adulthood you think?" I asked.

The landlord's face darkened, "never." He started to clean a clean a glass that was already spotless, he watched me down the pint and regretted having said anything. "Look we don't know what is going on up there; we tried to find out in the past but were warned off."

"Warned off?"

"Yes folk came here from somewhere, I reckons London, they weren't police and they weren't no soldiers, they were something in between. They told us never to go up there else they would kill us all and then Holt Fleet and Holt Heath would disappear from the maps just as the first Holt all those centuries ago."

"But they can't do that, two main roads run through these villages, and then you have all the river traffic, people would notice if all this went."

He interrupted me, "those kinds of men can do anything. If you are here to spy on us you can tell your boss that we don't care what's going on up there, we ain't interested."

"I'm not a spy," I tried to calm him.

He moved me away, "I don't care if you are if you are if you ain't, just keep your mouth shut that's my advice."

"That's normally good advice in most situations," I replied before sipping at the beer.

"Else they will kill you as well," the barman looked me in the eye before he turned away. I wanted to talk to him more but it was as if I was invisible and he even started acting as if he was alone, talking to himself at one stage.

I watched him as I drank that pint slowly before trying to start the conversation again: "If they opened the castle up there it would be great down here, you would get some visitors."

The barman never replied, it was as if he had not heard. I finished my drink and then walked down to the bridge, before crossing the road to watch the river thunder over the weir, there was nothing like it in London, old Father Thames was just that, an old man who just rolled past, there was no waterfalls or rapids or anything. I then looked over the fields onto the black and white cows grazing, everything was so normal here; I could almost believe that I had dreamt it all but it wasn't far up the bank to that other creepy world. I looked up the other side of the river and decided to take a walk, I thought of leaving the car there and walking forever. I had money, I could find myself some board in Birmingham maybe, get a job in a factory there, I smiled I would be better to throw myself into the river here and end it all now.

The road to Ombersley was up a steep bank that I should imagine was a death trap in the icy weather. It was ten minutes before my eyes met the village church with it's spire, it reminded me of Hallow, no doubt the family had paid for it to placate the natives. I don't really know what was going on in my mind as I walked towards it, past a row of small shops, which made the village look like a fledging town, all it needed was some coal to be found here and the place would be another Birmingham. I headed towards the church, maybe I would find some friendly vicar there and I would talk to him as I had once talked to the army chaplain, he had tried to make sense of things for me, but it was impossible to make sense of an inferno. I had known that on the other side of the lines German pastors and priests had been telling the enemy soldiers that they were fighting for God as well.

Ombersley was no place in the middle of nowhere, the main Worcester to Kidderminster road ran through it, most towns back then were famous for making one thing, for Kidderminster it was carpets. I had to wait as a lorry thundered past with a load of carpets on it's back. At the end of the street there stood a timber framed pub which had stood there before any of this. Folk said that Charles II had sheltered there after he escaped the Battle of Worcester, but there are a thousand places in England that claim the same thing, as if Charles had made some zigzag tour across the country before escaping to France. I then walked to the church like a ten year old going to Sunday school.

It was a typical English church, in England God seemed more suspicious and usually kept the doors to his houses locked, whereas he seemed to trust the French more, the Catholic churches there had always been open, even with a war raging outside. I was no Catholic but I found a beauty in them, something which called out to me, with their statues and paintings. The whitewashed churches of my youth had been sterile places where nothing could grow least of all faith. My eyes crossed the graveyard to a small chapel that looked older than the church itself, I walked over to it trying not to step on anyone's grave. I was right the chapel was far older than the church, above it's door there was a plaque which read, 'the vault of the Sandy's family.' Beneath it it read: 'Dedicated to the memory of Lord Sandys who stood at Wellington's side at the battle of Waterloo as his aide-de camp.' It seemed magical that I was so close to someone who had been at Waterloo, who had seen Napoleon finally crushed, but then hadn't I been at Marasesti? I was walking history myself. The Sandys were obviously the big shots around here, maybe they had been the ones who had paid for the church, maybe even they knew about the secret. The vault's door was sturdy enough and locked well enough as well, but when I looked around the side I could see windows that the putty could be picked out of easily enough and then the window opened. This place would be a good place to pass the night if needed, away from Donald and the Americans if we had to go it alone.

I headed back, through the graveyard, glancing over to the butcher's shop where Fitzroy often came to buy beef, the shop keeper stared at me, and something told me he had watched my journey over the graveyard. Ombersley was a big village, but a village all the same. As I headed back down the bank my eyes had settled on the car, a crowd had gathered around it. Some of course had never been close to a car before and such a car! It looked like it had been driven out of a film. I couldn't see how so many people had suddenly appeared, unless they had working in the fields or something, some of their clothes did seem to be caked in mud, but then they were probably like that anyway. "Is this your car?" One asked.

"No I am just the chauffeur," I replied.

"A chauffeur? And what's one of them when it's at home? Sounds like a Nancy boy to me."

The others laughed and I shrugged, "I'm the driver."

"You're from up at the castle now ain't ya?" Another stepped forwards.

I nodded, "yes I am working up there."

The crowd then drew forwards, "who lives up there then now?"

"Oh a couple from London."

The crowd gave an ooh in unison as if I had just said they were from Mars, the man who obviously was their spokesman edged forwards, "what are you doing down here then if you are from the castle?"

"I just thought that I would take a look around, I have never been in this part of the world before."

The yokel edged forwards, "where are you from?"

"London," I replied.

The crowd gave another ooh, I smiled, "have you ever been there?"

"No, of course not, I have never even been to Burningham and one thing for sure I know that I never will," he replied proudly.

I smiled, "well I must agree with you on that one."

"What were you doing over the river?"

I frowned, "just having a look around you know."

"They don't likes us over there," the man grunted, "they calls us Welsh."

"Well there is nothing wrong with being called that," I smiled weakly.

"Bloody cheek if you ask me," the yokel replied, "our ancestors died so that the people over there in Ombersley could continue eating their scones and drinking their tea. Now they look at us as if we are half-Welsh peasants when we cross the river to go to their church."

"Ignore them, that was a long time ago, we are all the same side now," I smiled.

"We stood against Glendower as well when he came here!" The man continued.

I stepped back, a little amazed at this humble man's knowledge, what similar person in London would know anything of that great city's past? "I knew a lot of Welshmen during the war, men from the mining villages of the south and from the farming villages of the north too, people who spoke Welsh amongst themselves and they were all good blokes."

Some of them scoffed at that, "you're not Welsh are you?" One man asked.

My first questioner then stepped forwards, "my son died out there in France, I never did know what all that was about?"

I paused, "no neither did I."

Maybe reading this in 1950 it seems like I mention the Great War over and over again, but that was the way it was in 1926, even places like this it had touched, even a place like Holt Castle cut off from the world for centuries it had entered. It was the sadness of our lives back then, of course since then there has been another war, and people no longer talk so much about that one, because everyone knows these so-called world wars are nothing special anymore and come about every twenty years.

I paused, "I'm sorry, I'd best go now."

I went to go into the car when the yokel stepped out in front of me, "look I don't know who you are, you say you are a Londoner, but still you seem alright."

"Thanks," I went to get into the car again.

He stepped in front of me again, "that place is no good."

"I'm sorry?"

The yokel looked straight into my soul, "that place up there is cursed, it has been cursed since the time of bad King John, if anything happens up there don't expect no coppers to go up there, or any of us, you are on your own."

I paused, there was no point in asking what he meant, I already knew, "alright, goodbye."

He nodded, 'yes God be with ye."

I started the car up and the yokel even turned the handle for me, something he must have seen in a film, the crowd scattered as the engine came to life, only edging back with caution. I knew that they would be talking about this for a long, long time; there wasn't much else to talk about amongst the cow pats of mid Worcestershire. The yokel then handed me the starting handle and looked me firmly in the eye, "may God protect you."

Donald was standing by the gate when I drove up to it, "where have you been?" He snapped.

"I was followed, I had to jump on a bus to Malvern," I lied.

Donald smiled, "there are worse places to go I guess. Who was it? The same people?"

I nodded, "I think so, it was a young guy this time, he didn't look American to me."

"There are many races in America," he replied, "a Chinaman can be an American."

"Yes but there was something different about this guy," I added.

Donald edged forwards, "in what way?"

"I don't know," I admitted, "some expression in his eyes."

Donald threw up his hands, as if I had finally lost the plot. "Well let's hope that there is only one group of them, I don't feel like killing too many people." He then cursed as he dragged the gate open himself.

Fitzroy hurried out and took the gate off Donald before scowling his eyes towards me, "it is a good job that you never got back any later, I was about to let the animals out!"

I drove inside, hiding the books inside my coat before handing the bags over to Donald as I got out, "where's the baby?"

"Upstairs with Matilda," he frowned.

"Might as well say hello," I replied.

"Yes why not?" Donald then looked down at the bags I had handed to him, who the hell was the servant around here me or him?.

"I don't like him," Fitzroy grunted.

Donald smiled, "do you even like me Fitzroy?"

"I don't know who you are, but I know who he is, trouble."

Chapter Eight: The secret is revealed.

Matilda had been sat on her bed, waiting, waiting like a blind girl to hear any sound that would say I was back, for an hour she been listening to the creaking of the floorboards, to Donald's and Fitzroy's raised voices downstairs, then Fitzroy's hissed voice when he talked to his wife. As soon as I entered the castle she rushed downstairs, clutching the baby of course, "oh thank God you are back."

I nodded before closing the front door behind me and then looking down towards the kitchen to where Mrs Fitzroy was preparing some food, "why what has happened?"

"Nothing, it's just they give me the creeps," she whispered.

Now I felt a little guilty for my little jaunt to Ombersley, and I had learnt very little through it, "don't worry I am back now." As we walked upstairs I smiled, "the Fitzroys obviously are as much a part of this as the castle itself, they've been so long here in this dark corner of the human race that it's normal to them now. I'd like to know what Donald Pembridge's past is though, I mean before I met him."

"He seems like one of those people who will do anything for the King," she replied letting me into her room without me asking.

I looked at her, "so you think it's definitely the King behind all this?"

She nodded, "I think so, this goes all the way back to them."

"You're probably right, you're probably right about Donald too, but he has his limit. He also has something which is dangerous inside the United Kingdom of Great Britain and whatever's left of Ireland," I replied.

"What's that?"

"An independent mind, he thinks about things, analyses them," I drew back and shrugged, "but of course it doesn't mean that he won't do the wrong thing at the end of it all. We can't trust him if that's what you were thinking, but then I think maybe they can't either."

"What did you get in Worcester?" She asked.

"Oh the usual things but then I had to go to the post office and picked up a message for him."

"What did it say?"

I smiled, "now didn't your mother say that it is rude to open other people's letters?" I smiled, "but I tried, you see the envelope was not sealed, but I couldn't make out much of it."

"Why?"

"It's not written in English," I replied.

"What language was it written in?" She asked.

"God knows, it wasn't French I know that, the thing it most looked like to me was Romanian," I replied.

"So he's working for the Romanians?" She gasped.

"I doubt it," I laughed, "I have never heard of a Romanian spy; I doubt they have such things." I then reached inside my coat and pulled out the books, "Alexander Dumas," I bowed slightly, "as requested my lady." I handed them to her before my eyes became stern, "best keep them hidden, whatever secret they hold Donald doesn't want us to know."

Matilda took the books and looked over their covers, "'the Three Musketeers' and 'the Man in the Iron Mask,' oh that sounds creepy, it must be that one, I will read that one first."

"How fast do you read?" I asked.

"Not too fast, but I doubt I will sleep much tonight."

I nodded, "yes I doubt I will either, give me 'the Three Musketeers' then, I will have a shot at it. I wish I had kept one of Donald's pistols."

"Why? Do you think they will do something to us, during the night?"

I shook my head, "I don't know but it's what I would do, a sleeping army can be wiped out in seconds."

"I don't know how much longer I can take this," she fretted.

"Its good money, but suddenly it doesn't seem worth does it?" I agreed, and then my voice sank to a whisper little above silence, "maybe I will try to cut a deal with the Americans."

"Can we trust them?" she asked.

"I don't know them really but looking from the outside they look like the most untrustworthy people on the planet."

"Why?"

"Well look at their history, they're a people who let us defeat the French for them but didn't want to pay their bit to the army so they turned on us. Then they jumped into bed with Napoleon, I mean we really had our backs to the wall then and again they wanted to throw the knife into it. Then of course I don't need to tell you about how they waltzed into the last war late when most of us had nearly fought ourselves out. The land they live on is stolen from people they wiped out; they seem like the worst people on earth, but…"

"But what?" She asked.

"We have no choice."

I went to leave before she called me back, "Charlie?"

"Yes?"

Her face became tenderer now, "Donald told me that you are married, is it true?"

I looked down, "yes I am afraid so."

Her face stung and she thought about slapping me I could see that, "then why did you go to kiss me out there?"

I looked at her; she had fallen for me, was it true? After years of being told by my wife that I was no good I had forgotten that actually I am quite handsome, "that was for Donald's benefit."

"For Donald's benefit?!" she exclaimed.

"Yes," I affirmed, "you went out to tell me something, it was best that he thought that we had some little romance or something, it obviously worked for him to tell you that."

She looked hurt again, "I thought you liked me."

I looked at her and smiled, "I do," I felt a cad in every vein of my body.

"If we leave, I mean if we take this baby and go, you will have to leave your wife, not to be with me but to-"

"I already have," I interrupted. She wanted me to kiss her, but I drew back, "I'd better go and give our master his message, I bet he's already getting worried about it."

"Yes," she nodded and looked away, I was about to leave when she looked up, "oh Charlie."

"What?"

"Thank you."

I smiled, "don't worry about it, we're in this together."

Matilda then listened to my footsteps as I headed downstairs. Donald was sat there at the table, sipping the brandy I had just bought him. Strange I couldn't remember him hardly drinking in Romania, he looked up at me, "how is she?"

"Fine."

He then nodded, "and the baby?"

"Yes she looks fine as well," I answered.

Donald almost wished the baby would die, that would solve the whole problem.

"Oh sorry I almost forgot I didn't give you the message I picked up in Worcester."

He flinched at the use of the city's name and then held out his hand, "give it to me." He took the unsealed envelope and then opened and read it, he frowned for a moment and then laughed.

"What does it say?"

"It's from Fitzroy, he certainly has his own form of Latin, but it's legible," he looked at it like a language professor.

"It says that he is undercertain about me, whatever that means, and that he suspects me of being a Bolshevik," Donald laughed.

I nodded, I had made that word out myself, "but why did he send it to you?"

Donald screwed the paper up and threw it into the fire, "he doesn't realize that I am his contact, I have been receiving his messages for five years before we came here."

I then changed the subject, "how did you get this job, Sir?"

He looked at me, and then shrugged, "well I might as well tell you."

'Yes maybe I will dead soon,' I thought.

"After we went our separate ways in Romania, and you became a Dacian warrior and I went to Russia well I became the middle man for us there. I was speaking to all sides. I had won over Kerensky.Oh he was a charming man," Donald reminisced, "a socialist but a charming one. I kept Russia in the war a few months longer, but maybe I shouldn't have because things became impossible for him and the devils took over, lead by that German agent Lenin. I never met Trotsky but I met Lenin and he told me that he wanted the Tsar and his family out of Russia; he wanted to send them packing. He gave me a message for the King; he would send a ship with them all on it to Southampton. If they stayed in Russia Lenin said he would kill them all. He just wanted them out of his hair, not that he had much of it. So I went to England with a message for the king, while his cousin the Tsar sat a prisoner in his own country. I set sail for England at once; a boat left Murmansk that very night and took me round the Kola Peninsula and down the coast of neutral Norway. I stood and looked out over the beautiful fjords, but I cursed them, I just wanted to get to England as quickly as I could. I had that family in my mind, those beautiful daughters and the little boy who had suffered so much in his life already. Of course the German woman they could have shot with my blessing, but the rest I had to save! We went across the North Sea and braved the U boats, in the distance I could see some ship aflame, but we never stopped the survivors could drown for all I cared. It was night when we arrived in London, and I went straight to the palace. I demanded to see His Majesty, I demanded of a King! He received me as if I was crazy man. Then I saw the face, the face which was so alike the one I was trying to save."

Donald then stood up and looked into the flames of the fire, "then he asked me what I wanted, what was so important. I said that I had news of his cousin. He replied, which cousin? He had many. I said the His Majesty the Tsar of all the Russias! You know what he said?"

"No," I prompted.

"He said that he had heard that he was no longer the Tsar of any Russias and that he had resigned, there was no humanity in his face at all," Donald lamented. "I said that I had news from Lenin, I said who Lenin was that he was a German agent, that he was a butcher. I said that unless we take in the Tsar's family he would kill them, and I told him that Lenin was serious, that to him life meant nothing, not the life of a peasant or a King. The King just looked at me and said that that must be very liberating for him. I said that his whole family would be killed; never let history say that I didn't plead for their lives with everything I had. It was as though the King never heard, he said he had no time to hear more of this nonsense and that he had to go back to bed. I shouted at him, at the King! He just waved me away. One of his courtiers then told me that the Romanovs day was over and it was best Lenin closed the chapter on them; I asked if he wanted me to tell Lenin that, he said yes and may God have mercy on their souls. Well of course you know the rest, a group of Latvians took the whole family and their servants down into the cellar and they shot them all."

"Doesn't that make you more a republican?" I asked.

Donald smiled, "it doesn't make me anything, I am doing a job, the palace liked my professionalism after that I passed the message onto Lenin and the family was all shot. That was my last act in Russia, our friends were losing the civil war and we were going to abandon Russia to the rule of the devil. I came back to London and carried on working for the palace, I never mentioned the Tsar again, even when I met the King, and I never told anyone this story, until now. They liked my professionalism that is why they have trusted me with this."

I nodded, "that is one hell of a story!"

He smiled, "that is life I guess, no Russians came here to save our King from Cromwell, so why should we have saved theirs?"

"Will you tell him?" I asked.

"Who?"

"Fitzroy, you know about the message."

Donald shook his head, "no, I like to know what people are thinking, he can send all the messages he wants."

I nodded, "I'll go to my room then Sir."

I was about to turn away when Donald added, "what are you thinking Simmonds?"

"I try not to Sir."

"What?"

"Think."

Night set in over holt Castle and plunged black the river Severn, the lights flickered from the inn where all the talk was of the Londoner, folk would have liked to say strange Londoner, but really apart from his accent there was little strange about him. Fitzroy looked towards those lights and wondered if they knew about all this, oh how he would love to pour petrol through their letter box and burn that place down. From her room Matilda could see those lights, twinkling through the branches, she held the baby to her breast. It seemed so easy just to head out through the back door and make her way towards the lights, then she saw one of the strange dog like animals move into the moonlight, it's shimmer etching out it's strangely striped back. She drew towards the window and the creature turned towards her, it's dark eyes staring into hers, like it was trying to tell her something, then it looked away. Her eyes then fell on the books and gingerly she lifted up 'the Man in the Iron Mask' and slowly drew back the cover before being taken into the Bastille of three centuries before. Her prison was different to that one, but it was a prison all the same. Of course like all novels it meandered a bit and she shouted at it to give her it's secret quickly.

From my room I looked down onto the strange dog like creatures, and I tried to guess how savage they were, they looked like dogs but would they act like them, were they pack animals? I could probably kick them off one at a time but if they all rushed on me I would be gone a million, then of course I would be heading across that courtyard holding a baby and dragging a woman behind me. Of course if I killed Donald and the Fitzroys that would solve everything, but what if I lost my nerve? It had been a long time since I had killed anyone, and of course I knew Donald wouldn't hesitate. I had to get my hands on the revolvers as well and I was sure that Donald wouldn't be leaving them just hanging around. Then of course it wouldn't be the end of the story, Donald worked for someone and they would come after us. One of the beasts yawned and his mouth opened almost 90 degrees, in a way no dog could making it look more like a crocodile. I felt a cold chill run through me and I had a taste for brandy myself. I headed downstairs but instead of Donald Fitzroy was sat in the Lord's seat while his wife cleaned around him.

"Mrs Fitzroy," I smiled, "it is late and the place is clean enough already."

Fitzroy smiled with pride, "my wife is like that, she hates dirt like a German hates peace."

"Where is Mr Pembridge?"

Fitzroy smiled, "he has just turned in for the night."

Simmonds nodded, "then maybe so should I."

Fitzroy laughed into the night, "you really don't know what the hell you have gotten yourself into do you?"

I nodded, "I can't argue with that."

Fitzroy kicked out a chair, "come join me Mr London. I know that you are a noble gentleman from the greatest city on earth and I am only a peasant from the backwoods of Caerwrangon but I hate drinking by myself. Of course we will have to avoid the Lord Pembridge's brandy but I have plenty of cider."

I smiled, "I'll drink anything."

"My sweet fetch Mr Simmonds a glass will ye?" he called.

Mrs Fitzroy planted a glass before me and then filled it up with a cider in which bits of apple floated , I took the glass and downed it like a Somerset farmer on a hot day before placing it down, Fitzroy chuckled, "I think our visitor from London requires another one my sweet, we are educating him." As his wife poured another glass his eyes settled on me like roasting coals, and he pushed aside the plate he had been eating off. "It was a nasty business in Russia wasn't it? I mean the King getting shot and all that."

I nodded, had he heard what I had been speaking to Donald about? "It happened here once, it was nasty but it will pass."

"I hope it does a people need a king, like sheep need a shepherd, but now they don't have one, the Germans don't either."

I smiled, "yes but they were probably better off without that scoundrel."

"Oh yes, yes to be sure, I would have shot that bastard! But a people need a king all the same. What are these people the Bolsheviks like? They are unruly sorts from the factories ain't they?" Fitzroy asked.

I smiled to myself, maybe I could use this fear to my own advantage, "some are, some are not, and some are posh folk from big houses."

Fitzroy's eyebrows rose, "really?"

"Yes of course," I leant back and took a gulp of the cider, I could almost get use to it. "Simple folk from the fields and the factories always need clever people from posh schools to lead them."

"I yeard that they plan to take over the world, they have already been chased out of Hungary, I" he leant forwards.

"Yes,"I nodded, the Romanians had chased Bela Kuhn out of Budapest they had saved Europe from communism and looted the city of everything they could carry.

"And in London, are they in London?"

I smiled, "sure they are Mr Fitzroy, they are in London, Birmingham even in Droitwich."

Fitzroy took a drink himself, "but how can you tell them apart? I mean from the rest of us."

"You can't Mr Fitzroy, you can't."

Fitzroy gulped his cider down as he imagined an army of Bolsheviks advancing over the fields of North Worcestershire towards the castle as the Welsh once had. This time though they wouldn't be repelled because the people around them would rise up, infected with Bolshevism themselves. If they could destroy the Emperor of all the Russias, what could they do to Holt Castle?

Above us Matilda turned the pages of Dumas, the meandering was not much between her and Aramis's conversation with the prisoner, slowly the musketeer revealed the secret, not just the secret of a long dead French king but the secret of Holt Castle. She heard of a baby taken from his mother as the baby she suckled had been, she read with fear as to how the nurse who had cared for him had been murdered, as no doubt she would be. Then she read the reason why all this had happened and the book fell from her hands, so that was it.

Renda's car headed north out of Worcester, Kuperstein drove, he was a blond haired Baltic German, a refugee from Memel, his family had left when the city had been invaded by the Lithuanians and given a name no one could even pronounce. He was in his twenties and confident, he smiled a lot and was sharply different to Kondrakov who sat in the passenger seat, but the two had become friends, more that that. "Where are we going?" Kondrakov sighed, "it is late."

Kuperstein looked in the rear view mirror and Renda leant forwards from the darkness, "that day Simmonds knew he was being followed, but he didn't know at first, I reckon he didn't know at first at least, when he figured it out he turned off, he took the Martley road, so we will take the other way."

Kondrakov sighed, he was tired, "maybe you are wrong Sir," he replied gingerly.

Renda snarled, "then I am wrong!"

Kondrakov jolted causing Kuperstein to smerk.

Renda then calmed down, "then I will have been wrong and we will have wasted our time and petrol, but we are achieving nothing sat in the Star Hotel. We will stop first in Hallow that is the first village, you two will go in there and ask if anyone has seen a car, and you will describe their car."

"They will want to know who we are," Kondrakov replied.

"You will tell them that you work for an insurance company and that the car has been stolen and that you are investigating."

"Is it not too late for that kind of thing?" Kondrakov moaned.

Renda shook his head and resisted the temptation to punch the Russian's cheek, "no this is the best time, the pub will be full and alcohol will loosen a few tongues. Ask too if there any big houses around here that a gang of car thieves might be using, a place that folk don't go to too much."

"But it is late for us to be working," Kondrakov replied.

"With the reward the insurance firm is offering you are prepared to look all night for it," Renda smiled.

"And what if we learn nothing?"

"Then we will go back to Worcester and I will wait there for news from Simmonds while you two try the next village on the road what is it?"

"There is a village down a track by the river called Grimley," Kuperstein replied looking at the map, "and the next one along this road id called Holt Heath, there is a crossroads there and the three roads from there."

Renda nodded, "well let's hope that we find something out before that crossroads, or that someone in Holt Heath can tell us which way they went." The darkness of the countryside fell around them, "it is strange how such a small and worthless island could build such an empire."

"They built an empire because they were an island, they could sail off and attack others but couldn't be attacked," Kondrakov replied. "For us Russians our sea was the land itself, anyone who wanted to attack us had to cross it before they could get to Moscow, and it was a sea full of attackers, and if they didn't get to our capital before winter then they froze."

Renda nodded, "yes there is that, but they were clever too once but not anymore. They showed that during our civil war, that was their last chance to come in and finish us off but because of their liberal values they sat there and did nothing, and we emerged from it stronger than ever."

The spire of Hallow church rose up into the dark night, this was a village that was always within an hour's walk of Worcester cross, but the further they advanced along that road the deeper they got into the countryside, the broader the accents became and the more they became the old Mercian border people that King Offa would have known. The village green bore a maypole opposite the inn. Kuperstein pulled up outside it and sighed before getting out, he was a little nervous; he just hoped that they didn't notice his slight German edges to his accent. Kondrakov got out as well, leaving Renda to look out over the night village. There is something idyllic about an English village, something that appealed to most Americans even those who didn't have even one drop of English blood. Renda's father had been Sicilian and had found his way to America after killing someone in Palermo,and then found his way to New Mexico after killing someone in New York. The local women had marveled at the way he had corrupted Spanish with his own language, smoothing over the ugly pronunciations with his soft Italian sounds. Renda looked about the village and soaked in the moonlight, but he knew that there were bastards everywhere, if he lived here he would quickly set the people against each other, he would sour the place totally.

The door cracked open and the night blew in and with it two old eyes stared out from a young face, crossing the pub with contempt, he despised English people really. Those eyes were the eyes of a man who had left his homeland and he knew that he would never see it again. There was hatred in those eyes for the people who sat in that village pub, in the place where they had always lived and their kin had lived for centuries, whereas he was a tramp, a man who had no home. Or maybe I am reading too much into it, Kondrakov just hated English people.

A silence fell over the pub, it was well past the time for outsiders to come here, "can I help you Sirs?"

Kondrakov said nothing before Kuperstein swept past him, "two beers please my good man."

"Come up from Worcester have you?" The landlord asked.

"Are you foreigners?"

"Yes, we are from London," Kuperstein smiled.

The landlord grinned at that, "well we'll try not to hold that against you. You know if I was king the first thing I would do is move the capital out of there and put it in Worcester."

"Really," Kondrakov sneered, "why?"

"Here in Worcestershire we are in the heart of the country, look at any map, Scotland is the head, Wales the arms , Cornwall the leg, Norfolk and Suffolk and all them stupid places are the bottom and London, well London is the asshole," the landlord declared and the whole pub erupted in laughter, of course they had heard him say it before but never to a Londoner. "Oh it's true!" He declared above the laughter, "look at any map and it will tell you." He then looked at them to see if he had riled them, he had nothing to worry about; he had a whole pub to back him up. Seeing that he hadn't annoyed them and actually they were chuckling themselves he drew back disappointed, "so what brings you here?"

"We are looking for a stolen motor car."

"Oooh hark at it," the landlord laughed, "a stolen motor car!"

The pub laughed again and Kuperstein chuckled, "have you seen any?"

"Cars pass here all the time, I know we're a long way from London, but there is a road outside and folk do use it," the landlord mocked.

Kuperstein nodded, "yes I guess so, what if someone though did steal a car is there any place around here where they could hide it, you know a place folk don't poke around too much."

"Like a secret place," Kondrakov added.

"A secret place," the landlord mused and rubbed his chin, "a place folk don't go to too much."

"Yes! That's right!" Kondrakov urged.

"Oh yes there is a place like that, the bloody Kremlin's just down the road!" The landlord laughed.

The pub all joined in but one man was getting to feel a bit embarrassed, "there is a place, but there are no stolen cars there."

"How do you know?" Kuperstein asked, finally receiving his pint and sipping at it.

"Because no one ever goes there."

"Why?"

The villager shrugged, "certain places you just stay away from you know. The people up in Holt know more about it, ask them, mind they don't like talking about it, but there is a haunted castle up there, that's what folk say, only it isn't haunted by ghosts but by men."

"Have you seen it?" Kuperstein asked.

The villager shook his head, "no, and it ain't marked on no maps either."

"Then maybe it is just all stories," Kuperstein replied.

"Maybe," the villager replied, "I ain't forcing you to go there. But you London folk said that about dragons, said it was all tommy rot and all that, but I read that the Dutch have an island somewhere in the East Indies where they found them! Oh they don't breathe fire but all the rest is true."

"If dragons are true maybe the haunted castle at Holt is as well," Kondrakov concluded.

The landlord then leant forwards, "your accents sound a bit off, you're not Americans are you?"

"No."

"Good, "the landlord nodded, "I hate Yanks."

Kondrakov looked back outside to where Renda sat and wished that he had been here to hear that, but then the landlord was just the kind of idiot he would laugh at and no more, "yes, you're not wrong there."

Chapter Nine: A decision is made.

Morning broke over the battlements and I woke up glad not to have Donald's gun leveled at me, I jolted and looked around the room, I must have been having a nightmare, but I couldn't remember what it had been about now. I looked out over the Worcestershire countryside, mist rolled over it, mist not the poisonous smog of London, but the kind of thing which felt fresh and damp when you breathed it in, maybe if I did nothing I could stay here forever, or maybe I could change the world, really make my mark on it, in a way none of my family ever had. No one in my family had ever written or invented anything, all my ancestors were now long forgotten, but I could be different, but then it wasn't about that. A knock came at the door and I pulled on a dressing gown, "please come in."

It was Matilda clutching the book as if it was her new bible.

"Good morning Matilda."

"Good morning Charlie," she smiled.

I then looked down at the book, "so you've read it then? Sorry I didn't get far with mine," in fact I hadn't even opened it.

"Only the first few chapters," she confessed, "but it is all there in chapter one, the whole thing!"

I smiled and wondered if she wasn't getting carried away a little, "well don't keep me in suspense then, what is it about?"

"A man is kept a prisoner in France, but he is no criminal, he has done nothing wrong, his only crime is to have the same face as the King of France."

"A pretender?" I replied, "but they always find those guys out, wasn't there some guy called Perkin Warbeck who caused trouble years ago, but they found him out."

"But what if he was exactly the same as the king, same face, same body, what if the scientists carried out tests, blood tests and found it was all the same," Matilda replied.

"But that's impossible," I scoffed.

"Not if they are identical twins!" She declared, "the King of France was a twin, one twin became King the other became a prisoner."

I frowned, "but why?"

"Because they don't want any rivals to the crown, and who could be a bigger rival than someone born at the same time as the king who looks exactly like him! Imagine if one day the younger twin claims that he is the older one, and no one can tell them apart!"

I drew back, "you think that that baby there is a twin, a twin of the Princess?"

"Why not? It's the only thing that makes sense!"

I thought about it and then shook my head, "ah it's just some novel some French guy wrote years ago, you know the French they are always talking nonsense."

Matilda nodded, "maybe it is, maybe it has all come off the top of his head, but then maybe he just hit on something by chance. Look think about it, when have you ever heard of a king who was a twin?"

"Never, I don't think," I confessed.

"How many are there in the royal family now?"

"None," I replied. "But what does that prove? There are no twins in my family it doesn't mean we have locked them all up in a castle somewhere."

"But have there never been any twins in the Simmonds family? Never going all the way back to Alfred the Great's days?"

"I don't know,"I admitted, "but it doesn't seem likely."

Matilda was now seized on the subject, "no it isn't, but we know about this family, we know about their ancestors! They are all buried in Westminster Abbey! No King has ever been a twin, ever! Is it bad luck? Or chance? It is not possible."

I shrugged; I wasn't as enthused as she was, "maybe not, so you think that that is what Holt Castle has always been used for? To keep the second twin, the younger one away from people."

"Yes! That is what *our* baby is!" She declared.

"Hey but look she is only the first child, I mean they could have more and more children, what if the next one is a boy, and then If I remember her father isn't even in line to be king there is an older brother, what if he has children?" I argued.

"Yes but what if he doesn't!" She countered, "what if our baby's twin ends up being the Queen some day? You can't have two Queens! They can't run that risk and even so her father isn't the Prince of Wales and is in line for nothing, but still they can't take the gamble do you see that?"

I nodded, "but why hide her away here?"

"What if our child grows up and is seen out in the streets, and she looks like the person you see on the bank notes?"

I waved her away with that one, "yes but there are people who look a bit like the King, you see them all the time in the music halls."

"Yes they look a bit like him but not exactly! This child will be the exact copy of the Queen," Matilda affirmed.

"Chances are she won't even be Queen," I repeated.

"Yes but they can't take that risk!" She repeated, getting a little frustrated with me, "that's why there are no twins anywhere in the royal family! We have certainly stumbled across a secret!"

"But then it is not such a secret if Dumas told the world about it centuries ago," I replied.

"Yes he told the world but people never thought about it, they never sat down and thought what if it was true, they thought it was just some legend that was kicking about France!" I had not seen her so passionate before, "Dumas could have done more to spell it out I suppose."

"Then he would have ended up in an iron mask himself," I quipped.

"But at least they won't do anything to this child," Matilda added, "she is of their blood."

"She is also surplus to requirements," I replied, "if what you saying is true. It is all about the heir with these people, he gets everything and the others go to hell. They do not think as we do, any normal family wouldn't have done to Europe what they did, they wrecked us, wrecked us all," and for a moment I was back there in the hell of those years.

Matilda saw this, she had seen that look before in the eyes of her father and she took my hand, knowing it was all she could do, because she had not been there.

I sighed, "looks like I need to speak to the Americans."

"What can they do?"

"They will give us a new life over there in California or Kansas or wherever, there is even a place called Worcester there," I smiled.

"I wonder what Donald calls that place," Matilda laughed.

"We'll avoid it anyway," I smiled, "I think I have had enough of this Worcester, I hardly want to see another one."

Her eyes then drew wide and tender, "what about your wife?"

I looked away, "it was over before I even came here Matilda, it is nothing to do with you, or the baby or anything, the marriage is dead."

"Why?"

I sighed, "my wife made the big mistake of marrying someone who she was not just not in love with but never loved at all."

"A man's place is with his wife," she chided.

"Not every marriage is like it is in the fairy stories," I betrayed my sadness in my eyes.

"But you loved her when you married her?" Matilda tried again.

"I thought I did, but she never loved me," I had to change the subject; "look you'd better get back to your own room before Donald thinks that we are doing something in here."

"Doing what?"

I smiled again, "what do you think?"

She blushed before I opened the door for her and she headed back to her Bastille. I didn't find her that attractive, but certainly she made me feel handsome again, for the first time in a long time, I guess fate threw us together not love.

I got dressed and headed to the courtyard where Fitzroy was rounding up the last of the beasts; my eyes fell on Mrs Fitzroy, "I don't think that I have ever seen animals like that before."

"Neither will you either," she snapped, "there are none like them in the whole of England, they have come from the jungles of Van Diemen's land, you will have to go there and see another."

"Have you seen much of the rest of England Mrs Fitzroy?" I asked.

She shook her head, "not much, when my sons said that they would go to France it seemed like they were going to the edge of the earth."

I nodded, "it seemed like that to me as well, the last land before hell."

She then looked at me, and her voice seemed on the edge of tears, "you were there weren't you Mr Simmonds?" She never waited for my reply, "I mean what was it like? My boys said that it rained a lot."

"It rained alright; it rained for days on end. Our dug out was flooded most of the time and we slept out in the rain sometimes."

"It is amazing what men will suffer for their King," she replied.

"Some didn't, some mutinied, they had had enough and they were shot for it," I replied.

Her eyes fell on me with doubt, "how do you know all that? It weren't in the papers."

"I was there my lady," I lamented.

"What you mutinied?" she snapped.

I smiled, "if I had I wouldn't be here, because they were all shot."

"How do you know then?"

"I was in the firing squad, I tell myself I fired wide, but I never, I hit him, if I hadn't I would have been up there next as a mutineer, one English wife or mother cried her eyes because of my bullet," I shrugged.

"More like Irish," she snapped, "they were the ones rebelling in the streets."

"No they were English, they had just done enough for their King and they just had done enough," I retorted.

"They would have been better off under the last family," she retorted.

"The last family?" I frowned.

"The family that came from Scotland who Queen Elizabeth left her throne to, the Stuarts," Mrs Fitzroy replied.

"The Stuarts?" I frowned again.

She nodded, "yes she never left it to no Hannovers," she then looked away. "Good morning Mr Pembridge."

As she walked away Donald turned to me, "what was she talking about?"

"The Stuarts," I replied.

Donald gave a knowing smile, "just as I thought."

"What do you mean?" I asked.

"Remember when I said that Fitzroy's problem was different,"

I nodded.

"I reckon they are Jacobites, have you ever heard the word before?" Donald asked.

"Yes," I replied, "it was some lot of trouble makers up in Scotland."

Donald smiled, "what Bonnie Prince Charlie? It was a lot more than that, thousands followed him, from all over the kingdom, they came south into England and got as far as Derby before they were driven back and the cause died at the battle of Culloden, Stuart fled to France and never came back, but there are still people who follow it, not many but I think that the Fitzroys are amongst them."

"What is it?"

"They don't believe the King should be on the throne, they have their own King, a descendant of the Stuarts," Donald smile showed that he had only contempt for them.

"How deep is Fitzroy into it all?" I asked.

"I doubt very deeply, I doubt he knows anyone else, it is more he is a sympathizer."

"Is that a problem?" I asked.

Donald looked away, "it might be. Simmonds I'd like you to go out for me agin."

"Yes, I'll start the car up," I was keen to get out of there, but then I thought that maybe they were getting me out of the way so that they could do something to Matilda.

"No leave it," Donald replied, "I only want you to go to Ombersley, Fitzroy is a resourceful fellow, but there are some things here he can't make, and one goat is no longer enough for five of us drinking milk."

I looked back towards the castle, but Matilda couldn't be watching me because her window looked out onto the river. Donald looked at me, "so are you going or not?"

I nodded, I might as well get this over and so I headed out, I picked my way along the mud track, jumping over the puddles. I looked out over the apple orchards with sheep grazing in between the trees. In a way I didn't miss London, it wasn't natural for people to be herded into brick caves and forced to breath in smoke. In London though there was always an alleyway to duck down if you got into trouble and you could hide yourself in the confusion, here there was only fields, fences and hedges, a demon could chase you for miles here. I walked down towards the river, not paying much attention to the car parked in front of the pub, until it sounded it's horn. I turned expecting to see some Worcestershire idiot instead my eyes met the dead eyes again and my heart thumped heavily as Kondrakov stepped out, "good morning Mr Simmonds."

"What are you doing here?" I stammered.

Kondrakov's face cracked in a smile, "more to the point Mr Simmonds what are you doing here?"

"I,I-" I tried to think of a lie.

Kondrakov shook his head with a smile, he then tilted his head up towards the castle, "don't bother to lie, we already know it all, the whole story. Now it is you underestimating us, our Mr Renda wants to see you, he is inside," he nodded towards the pub.

I looked up the steep bank towards Ombersley and then back to the castle, I then nodded, "alright I'll talk to him."

As I walked back into the pub the landlord greeted me with an uneasy smile, "ah my friend from London."

I nodded, "good morning."

When I headed towards Renda the landlord nodded, he had known the minute the American walked in here that it had been Holt Castle business, he had that exotic weirdness about him. He couldn't place the accent, he saw Americans every week at So John's picture house but no words ever came out of their mouths. Renda was eating a huge steak and looked up at me in triumph, "good morning Mr Simmonds."

"Good morning," I replied coldly, "how did you find me?"

"You took the Martley road the day we were following you, so the Whitley road had to be the one you were meant to take, we didn't have to travel far up it until we started hearing village myths about this place. Normally I wouldn't listen to horse crap, but when you don't have anything else to go on you have to."

"Where did you find the charmer outside?" I asked.

He smiled whimsically, "why do you like him? If you do you might be in luck, I have my suspicions about him."

I ignored him and sat down, "maybe the time for hidden castles and mysteries has gone."

Renda then leant forwards, "you know Mr Simmonds you belong with us, and you are one of us."

I shrugged, "whatever you say, I am only here because you're the only people I can go to."

Renda smiled broadly, "what do you know about this baby?"

"Probably about as much as you do, it's all guess work really, the baby is a Princess, no doubt the twin of the one born a few months ago, who maybewill be Queen one day," I looked past him and out of the window towards the river, this was the interview where I would betray my country, is this how all traitors started?

"Maybe not I'm sure her uncle will have children, I have heard that he is quite the ladies man," Renda smiled, "but then I have heard that he is a man's man as well. Can we get your man Donald to come over to us maybe?"

I shrugged, "maybe, but it will take time, time we don't have."

"Why?"

"You being here has put the baby in danger," I replied. "I don't know if they are going to panic."

"You mean kill the baby?"

I nodded, "well that would make it easy for them, dump the body in the river, and it come ashore in Gloucester or some place down there and people will say it was some unmarried mother getting rid of her problems."

Renda shook his head, "you know where I am from when a woman gives birth to twins it is a big thing and she parades around like the Queen of Sheba, but your royals are more like some primitive African tribe who kill twins at birth. They are living in the dark ages, they belong in the history books, the only safe place for this child is America."

"Yes of course," I mocked, "they can get to us there, they can send people over, drive down from Canada, they don't even need a passport."

"It's possible, but this child is very important to us, she is the ace up our sleeve." Renda's eyes fixed on me, I think he was impressed that I didn't seem afraid of him, but then I wasn't a kid like Kondrakov. I met his stare and then looked away with disinterest:

"And what about me and Matilda?"

"Is that the maid?"

I nodded.

"You will stay with the baby."

"Really?" I replied sarcastically, "once you have got what you want you'll hang us out to dry."

Renda chuckled, "you really don't trust anyone do you?"

"Every time I do I get shat upon," I moaned.

"Not this time Mr Simmonds, we need you, and you are our witnesses, what if all this comes out, what will the British say? They'll say that we made her in a laboratory or something, but you are our witnesses, you can tell the whole story, about the creepy castle on the hill, about the creepy people living there, about what happened to Howard."

"Howard?" I frowned.

"Defford," he replied with a smile, "how did you see through him?"

"He was too smart for a country bobby, our boys have got uniforms going back not just years but decades, maybe the police in your country look like that but not here and he couldn't ride his bike very well, it was all very amateurish really," I mocked.

Renda's face flashed with temper but he decided to bury what he was going to say.

"You know all this would make a traitor," I moaned.

The New Mexican smiled, laughed at me the simple man with his flag and his king, "depends how you look at it, you know in your heart I am not going to do anything to harm that baby. It is not because I am saint but because that baby is important to us. You also know what they will do, they will kill her if they want to, you know that that baby is of royal blood, descended from King Alfred and all that."

"I am still a traitor."

Renda looked at me, "what is worse to be a traitor or a baby killer?"

"You'd kill her too if your president gives you the order."

"The difference is I will never get that order, we're going round in circles now Mr Simmonds," Renda sighed.

"Say if we get away, say if we are in America, the three of us living in a little cottage in Pasadena, how do I know that they would not get at my wife and kid?" I replied.

"What the one in London?" He smiled again like a Cheshire cat, showing that he knew so much about me.

"Yes,"I replied unimpressed.

Renda smiled, "not if we have the baby, they would be too afraid to."

I didn't need to be too clever to know that Renda was a gangster, between him and Donald I preferred Donald, at least he tried to be a gentleman, but I had no choice, "what do you want me to do?"

"Get the baby out of there and we will do the rest, it will go like clockwork," he smiled.

I nodded and rose to his feet, "you'll be caught and be deported and I'll go to prison for a very, very long time."

"Even without the baby we still have the story," Renda replied, "relax, your troubles are over. We are the Americans, we're dealing with it now, we can do what we like, wipe out whole tribes, whole races, massacre whole islands and we always come out smelling of roses."

I drew back, "what do you mean?"

"I was a soldier myself," Renda smiled, "not in that business you were involved in. I was in a proper war, not a war where you attack someone and they attack you, a war of two even sides, no this was a proper war. This was a war when a great, well armed white army fought against a poorly armed group of brown people. I was in the Philippines," he rolled the name out like it was paradise, "we fought together against the Spanish, we were brothers fighting side by side, then when the Spanish were driven out we turned on our smaller weaker brother. We were going to liberate them, only they didn't want to be liberated, we were going to make them Christians, only they already were Christian, they already went to church every Sunday with their white shirts. So they said no to us, you know what these Pacific island banana eaters are like?"

"Actually I don't."

Renda shrugged, "well of course we had to make them see the light of our type of Christianity. Oh we had to kill a lot of them, they are only little people but they are brave and fight like tigers, they kept coming at us, we would kill the father, and then his brother would come at us, then his son, then his younger son, until we were fighting children. Oh we had to kill a lot of them, about a quarter of the people we were trying to liberate. I was on the island of Samar, a fairly big island as they go over there, you know what we did there?"

"No."

"We shot every male over the age of ten," he sank back in his seat and smiled broadly.

"So you shot ten year old boys?" I asked,

"Me? Ten?" Renda mocked, "no of course not, but I shot plenty of eleven year olds. That quarter of the country we killed were it's best people, it's bravest, the ones that were left were the ones who dug the graves for us, the ones who gladly gave their daughters to us, the ones who accepted our benevolent protection. You know we did all that to a Christian people and no one said anything, you people did a lot less in South Africa and it was all over the world. That is the difference between us and you Simmonds. Get the baby to us and you can have a new life in America, bringing the baby up as your own."

At that moment, as if on cue, the landlord came over with a glass of wine, "sorry to intrude Sir."

Renda almost snapped, 'well don't then,' until he saw the drink, "what's that for?"

"You're American aren't you?"

"Sure am."

"I'd like to offer you a glass of blank, on the house, as a thank you for what you people did in the war," the landlord then bowed slightly.

Renda looked at me and winked, "that's alright my good man, someone had to finish it." With that he downed the wine as if it was beer before handing the glass back to the landlord, "thank you."

"No thank you Sir," with that the landlord backed away.

Renda then looked at me, "you see we always come out smelling of roses."

"That's wine probably poisoned," I muttered.

Renda grinned broadly, "it's never poisoned. No that wine tasted like piss to me, but to him it was a big thing, he was saving that behind the counter for someone special and here I am! Someone probably brought it back from the war for him and it has been there ever since."

I got to my feet, the whole thing had seemed staged to me, "I will have to talk to Matilda and think it over."

"Don't think too long though, else we will be coming up to get her ourselves," Renda warned.

"I guess you will be staying here now?"

"Yes I have a room here, I prefer it to the Star Hotel, it has great views of the castle," he smiled. I was about to go when he added, "you know in the Philippines I buried a man alive once."

I looked into his eyes and knew that that was true, "you planning to do that with me?"

He smiled, "not you, but maybe Donald."

I bowed, "goodbye Mr Renda."

"Let us say more *au revoir*," he smiled.

I walked out, he had succeeded in the end of unnerving me, I paused only to give the landlord a sideways glance, "Holt Castle business," he murmured still drying glasses.

Kondrakov watched me leave, his eyes gave me an icy expressionless expression, like looking into the eyes of a corpse. Kuperstein was stood on the bridge looking into the dark of the river, "*guden morgen mein herr,*" he smiled.

I nodded, "yes and the same to you."

Kuperstein's laughing blue eyes then followed me as I walked up the bank, "do you think he will do as we wish?"

Kondrakov nodded, "yes he will do what we want, he isn't the kind to kill a child." The Russian's eyes then joined his friend's in diving into the river, "you know rivers are the same everywhere, this reminds me of a river back home in Russia. I remember standing on a bridge there and watching the bodies float by, I even knew some of them." He chuckled a little.

Kuperstein looked at his frozen face, "do not worry brother we will see those days again."

The two retreated back to the car and watched me as I headed up to Ombersley and then watched as I headed down the bank again weighed down by two heavy bags. Kuperstein smiled as he read my lips murmur curses, "look at him he would never get into the German army, we had the best army in the world."

"You still lost," Kondrakov replied.

"Only because of two things," Kuperstein smiled, "we were outnumbered and the Jews."

Kondrakov frowned, "the Jews?"

"Yes they stabbed us in the back, everyone knows it, when our men were out there fighting they were wrecking things for us at home."

"Is that so?" Kondrakov replied. "The Jews were on your side, they all spoke German, the ones in Russia did anyway."

"Yiddish is not German," Kuperstein snapped.

"The Jews welcomed you with open arms when you came into the Baltic lands, they cheered," Kondrakov mocked.

"Only because you were so beastly to them," Kuperstein replied.

As I walked towards them Kondrakov shook his head, "look at him humble British Tommy, only ever good against a black man with a spear in his hand."

I looked up, "tell your boss to hold tight, the next time I go out in the car Matilda and the baby will be with me."

Kuperstein nodded, "yes I will tell him."

"The Jews were on your side, they always have been, it was us they didn't like," Kondrakov grumbled.

Chapter Ten: Grim town.

Donald sat in the lord's chair and stared into space, he was bored already, but then this would soon all be over, another Pembridge had lost another castle. This castle had passed down from one lord to another and he would be the first to lose it, he looked down at the pistols and thought of blowing his brains out, but that was always the easy way out. Fitzroy watched him and paused before he edged in and tried again, "so what was it like in Russia?"

"I'm sorry?"

"You were over there weren't you?"

Donald nodded, "yes so I was."

"It's the devil's business to kill your own king!" he repeated.

Donald looked at him and then smiled, he was sick of Fitzroy but maybe it was his time to have some fun, "we did the same here, we did it to Charles Stuart."

"Yes but, we have a King now," Fitzroy retorted.

"Not a Stuart king," Donald smiled, "the king we have is not from the same family as the family that Englishmen fought for and died for around here. He is a false king, an impostor."

"What do you mean?" Fitzroy squawked.

Donald nodded, "you know when Ireland went it's own way the protestants of the northern six counties wanted to stay with us. They call themselves loyalists and dress in orange, but the strange thing is they were the traitors. At the battle of the Boyne the Irish Catholics fought for the rightful King of England, King James Stuart, the man descended from the Kings of Scotland and the people who now call themselves loyalists fought for the usurper William of Orange, a Dutchman," Donald said the word with a sneer. "When the Americans rose up in rebellion the Protestants were on the rebel's side, the Catholics were on ours! Now they call themselves loyalists and the other side are republicans and traitors"

"What are you talking about?" Fitzroy asked.

"What I am saying my dear Fitzroy is the real King is living in France somewhere. That's what you think anyway isn't it Fitzroy?" Fitzroy was bubbling to come back but then I entered with the shopping, "ah Charles, how is Ombersley?" Donald asked.

"People stare a lot over there," I replied.

"People don't look at me at all," Fitzroy chuckled, "they are afraid of me over there, they can never meet my stare."

"Do they know what this castle is?" I asked.

Fitzroy never answered but Donald looked up at me, "do you?"

Simmonds paused for a moment, "no, but they have had more time to figure it out than I have."

"What do you mean?" Donald looked at me as cold as an executioner. For a moment there was an uneasy silence, and Donald repeated his question, "what do you mean? What is this place used for then?"

I knew there was only one game I had to play now, and I drew in a deep breath before launching myself into my bluster, "I am not sure, but what I am sure about is that you are both traitors!"

Fitzroy got to his feet. "What are you talking about?"

"Well this man is a Jacobite!" I rounded on Fitzroy, "he's waiting to betray the King, our King and have some Frenchman put in his place and you, you Sir are a Bolshevik!"

"You're crazy!" Donald spat.

"You were in Russia, working for Lenin, you told me yourself!"

"Is that true?" Fitzroy snapped.

"Ask him yourself! Ask him if it isn't true! He was there! He met Lenin! He's been a double agent all the time, he betrayed the Tsar! He helped the Russian front collapse and cost thousands of British their lives when the Germans in the east came back to fight us!"

Donald then got to his feet, "that is ridiculous!"

"You betrayed him! You told me yourself, you thought I was the same as you! Well I ain't, I ain't nothing like you! I ain't no bloody communist, I just said that to keep you going," I faked anger well enough, with that I strode out and slammed the door behind me.

Donald wanted to follow me before Fitzroy stepped out in front of him, "where do you think you're going Lord Pembridge?"

I heard Fitzroy's voice rise behind me as I headed upstairs, I had lit the blue paper now I had to get as far away from the explosion as I could.

Matilda opened the door and ushered me inside, "what is going on downstairs?"

I looked down to where the voices were getting louder and my voice sunk to a whisper, "I think they are onto us."

"What do you mean? Is that what they are shouting about?"

I smiled, "no that's what happens when a Trotskyist meets a Jacobite. They know that we have figured it all out, so we don't have much time, I have already spoken to the Americans."

Matilda frowned, "you have? But how?"

"They are here, down there in Holt Fleet."

"So close?!"

I nodded, "yes and I think that they have read their Dumas as well."

"Are they going to help us?" she pressed.

I nodded, "oh they'll help us alright."

"Maybe we are imagining all this, after all there was an Albino king once wasn't there?" Matilda replied.

"Edward the Confessor," I smiled, "I don't really know much history, but as a child I was taken round Westminster Abbey, and that was one of the things I was told. But you have to ask yourself Matilda how long ago was that? I mean 1060 something at least. An albino is not the same thing, a King can have pink eyes, that is not a problem, if there is only one King, they even made him into a Saint. Look if you want no part of this, I can deal you out of it, I'll do it all myself."

"No I am not saying that I am with you," her eyes showed me something my wife's never had, she was with me, she loved me, I could trust her.

I looked away, "no stay here, they won't do anything to you once I and the baby have gone."

"You don't know that!" She replied.

"Stay here," I replied more firmly, "it is safer here!"

"No, you need me!"

I nodded, yes that was true, "I don't know how to get away from those three."

"Maybe Donald wouldn't do anything," Matilda hissed."I mean maybe he wouldn't use the gun."

"You didn't see him at Dunstall," I replied."We could take the car, when I go out you could come out and get inside and then I step on the accelerator as hard as I can."

"You couldn't go fast along that track, Donald would catch us," she warned, "and he's the one with the guns, you're not."

I nodded she was right.

"If we did get away with it, if we did make it to America, I would never see my mother again."

"And I would never see my son," I added.

"Maybe she could visit me, I mean over there," Matilda hoped.

I shook my head, "she would be followed all the way from Southampton right to our front door. It is best you stay here."

"No," she shook her head, "I am coming with you."

I then walked over to the window and looked down to the river, to a small jetty jutting out into the water where a rowing boat was tied up, "what is that for?"

"Oh the boat? Fitzroy uses it to fish sometimes."

"Maybe we should take a longer look at it," I replied and opened up the door to where Fitzroy's voice was still raised:

"Socialism isn't natural I tell you!"

"Neither is feudalism, where there is a lord and serfs," Donald replied, "that is what it was like in Russia, it was like this country was in the middle ages that is why the people rebelled."

"I thought you'd support scum like that," Fitzroy mocked.

Simmonds flagged Matilda forwards, "bring the baby," he hissed.

"Are we going?" She asked.

"Seems like as good a time as any," I replied.

"But I haven't packed," she bleated.

I just laughed at that, lightly we tip toed down the stairs, but we didn't have to as the argument get even more heated:

"Your problem Fitzroy is that you have lived in this castle too long, you do not know what the world outside is like!"

"I know that I left two sons dead out there and I blame your Mr Hannover for that!"

I looked towards the kitchen and we edged out as Donald started to talk about the Stuarts again, how they would never come back. My hand lightly settled on the door handle of the back door and then I pulled it open. The baby was about to cry out when Matilda pulled out her breast and guided the baby's head towards it, I didn't know where to put my eyes. "What are they arguing about?" Matilda whispered.

I smiled, "Fitzroy thinks that Donald is a communist."

"And is he?"

"I wouldn't have thought so, if he was he would driven this baby straight to Russia."

"But they kill Princesses," she argued.

"They wouldn't kill this one," I retorted, although I didn't know that, there was no logic to who they were killing over there now.

We stepped out into the back garden and looked over Fitzroy's neatly kept vegetable garden which had been largely feeding them all their lives, it looked like one out of gardening book, not that I have ever read any.

Matilda's eyes settled on the rowing boat with uncertainty, "have you ever rowed before?"

"Never," I admitted, "but there can't be much to it."

"Don't forget that they have guns," she warned.

"Yes and we have the US Marines waiting for us up at Holt Fleet," I replied. Then I looked at her uncertain face, I felt like telling her to go back, but I didn't fancy handling a baby and a rowing boat together. "Come let's go."

"We're going now!?" she gasped.

"I'm not waiting for them to kill the baby first," I snapped and strode down towards the boat. Matilda followed, gripping the baby close to her breast. I looked back, hopefully they would be locked into that argument for a long time.

Fitzroy had finally showed his hand, "James Stuart was the rightful king! The king who had been chosen by God himself! You cannot say that it was wrong for parliament to give us Cromwell but it was right for them to force William of Orange on us, parliament doesn't decide who is the King!"

"James Stuart was a Catholic!" Donald countered.

"Who cares?! He was the King! It didn't matter if he was a Catholic, a Pagan or a Jew, he was the King!" Fitzroy shouted.

"That's some argument," Matilda gasped.

"Yes it's been bubbling up for some time," I agreed. "Now keep going!"

We hurried down the almost perfectly straight garden path, "are they coming?" Matilda asked.

I glanced back, "no, not yet!"

"Where are you going?" I turned as Mrs Fitzroy emerged form a vegetable plot. I strode towards her, in the last moment her face flashed with fear, but it was too late as I punched her and she staggered back, clutching her broken nose.

"What are you doing?" Matilda gasped in horror as Mrs Fitzroy writhed in the cabbages, blood pouring out from between her fingers.

"She was going to cry out," I explained, "now come on."

"You hit me you bastard," Mrs Fitzroy whimpered.

"Shut up else I'll fucking kill you!" I shouted back.

As Mrs Fitzroy got to her feet I got inside the boat and untied it, I glanced back to her, I must be losing my touch that punch should have knocked her out, unless she was a tougher old bird than I had at first thought. Matilda then hesitated, looking at me like she didn't know me anymore, behind her Mrs Fitzroy cried, "you forking bastard! You broke my nose."

"Get in the boat or stay here!" I snapped at Matilda. That spurred her forwards and my hands guided her down into the boat before I kicked it away form the bank and then began to battle against the current. It was obvious that I had never rowed before, but what I lacked in technique I made up for in brute strength.

"What are we doing?" Matilda gasped.

"You know what we are doing?" I snarled.

Matilda looked back at Mrs Fitzroy feeling her way around her as the world seemed to spin, "you could have killed her."

"It don't look like I'm that good," I replied as I fought against the current, Holt Fleet didn't look that far, but it could have been the other end of the Amazon the way I rowed. "What's she doing now?"

"She's running back to the house!" Matilda gasped.

I then cursed at the oars and sank them deeper into the water.

"You hit a woman a woman," Matilda tried again.

"I've killed a man before now," I replied.

"When?"

"In the war, I killed a lot, a regular hero I am, no doubt I'll burn in hell forever because of it though," I snapped, "can you see the pub?"

"Yes."

"That's where's the Americans are," I gasped, "at least I hope they are, or else we're in trouble."

'You are,' Matilda thought. She then looked beyond the bridge to the weir, "I never knew all this was here!"

"You never would have saw it either," I replied. "They would have kept you inside that castle like a prisoner."

I steered the boat towards the shore, trying to look back, expecting to see Donald emerge and start shooting, if he did he would hit us because as I remembered he was a good shot. I looked back up to the pub, "is there a car there? Is there a car there?"

"Yes," Matilda confirmed."Just use one oar, you will direct it like that!" She explained as I fought to get it near the shore, then she let out a cry.

"What is it?"

"There's another car coming down the hill, it's them!"

"I'll head for the bridge!" I snapped.

"I thought your Americans had guns!" She blurted.

"They do have, but we're sitting ducks out here." I just made it under the bridge as Donald's car stopped above us, I then reached out and gripped the weeds growing on the bridge's stone, but I uprooted them and the boat slipped back before I grabbed the stonework itself.

Above I could hear Fitzroy shout, "where are the bastards? Where are the bastards?"

I could feel my grip giving way as the river fought to take the boat with it downstream, "grab something," I pleaded.

"What?" Matida of course had the baby in her arms.

I looked to the edge of the bridge as if there was a guillotine there waiting to come down on us.

"I don't know they must have gone down stream," Donald replied, "but which side?"

"Grimley," Fitzroy snapped, "they won't want to go into the middle of the river, I bet a Londoner like Simmonds don't know one end of an oar from another!"

"Then we must go to Grimley, and get there before them!"

We then heard the car's engine start and pull off, and I let go of the bridge, and nursed my fingers and leant back in relief, but then I heard a second engine start some distance away, and I heard Kondrakov shout at his friend to get inside. As I got on the shore I saw Renda's car disappear up the bank, "damned that was them!"
"You mean that they have gone?!" Matilda gasped, "after all that!"

I climbed ashore and tied the boat up before drawing back to Matilda and helping her ashore, taking the baby in my arms for the first time and then looking down on her angelic face.

"Maybe they will come back," Matilda gasped.

"Yes hopefully we will be far away by then."

She looked down at my hand which was still speckled with Mrs Fitzroy's blood, "how could you do something like that?"

"I have done worse than that," I confessed.

We then walked towards the pub and I put my arm around her, "I just hope that Renda is there, otherwise we'll have to make our way cross country."

"But to where?"

"Not to Worcester that's for sure, that is the first place they will go to," I replied. "Maybe Droitwich, I think there is a train station there."

"Maybe we are wrong," Matilda started again, "I mean if there were twin sisters in the royal family, everyone would love it, they would be famous, they would be like film stars."

"Yes but who would be Queen?" I replied.

The landlord's jaw dropped as I entered, "good day Sir," he then looked at Matilda and then the baby and he dropped the glass he was drying.

"Is he here?" I asked.

The landlord pointed to a corner where I had met him before, he was still there, eating another steak. His attention had already been drawn to the breaking glass and he got to his feet as we approached, his eyes settling on the baby, "is that who I think it is?"

I nodded, "now it's time to do your part."

"Come on, let's get into the car!"

I then smiled, "there is a problem there, your car has just gone up the road after Donald's car."

"Damned idiots!" Renda cursed, "where have they gone?"

"Grimley, that's where Donald was heading anyway," I replied. "if they had been looking downstream towards the castle and not up at the pretty waterfall then they would have seen us escaping."

"Young fools!" Renda cursed then headed over to the bar, "where can I get a taxi?"

"Taxi," the landlord frowned as if he had never heard the word before.

"Yes a taxi, I need a taxi!"

"This is the countryside," the landlord explained, "this isn't Pasadena, there are no taxis here."

"Is there anyone with a car then?"

"Only them folk up at the castle," the landlord replied.

"Shit!" Renda spat.

The landlord's eyebrows rose as if he had never heard that word uttered before in Holt Fleet.

"We're deep in the middle of nowhere!"

"Why don't you just wait for your young men to come back?" The landlord asked.

Renda wanted to shout at him and he could feel the fury rising in him, he began to see him in a blur, but he drew back and bit his lip, "what about a boat then?"

"The lock keeper has one, but he won't be back til five, he went up river to Shrewsbury."
"How about a lorry then?" Renda pressed.

"No I am afraid not Sir," the landlord apologised, "you really are in a hurry to leave us."

"Yes you're right there!" Renda's face flashed with fury, he could have killed the man but he quelled the fire inside him and strode back to his table, pulling out his pistol to check it.

Matilda drew back, "does everyone have one of those round here?"

"You don't have a spare one do you?" I asked.

"I'm afraid not. Why does everyone in this stupid country go on about Pasadena? I mean it's not even a big place?!"

"It's because of that song," I replied."It was very popular here. So what's your plan?"

"We wait here," Renda replied.

"You're joking," I gasped, "after we have done all that to escape we are just going to sit about here!"

"My men will come back here," Renda seemed calm enough.

"What if they don't, what if Donald comes back?"

"Then we'll have to take his car then."

"I wouldn't underestimate him if I was you."

Renda looked up at me, "I wouldn't underestimate me either!"

Grimley is Worcestershire's secret village, it lies at the end of a road which goes nowhere, a road which leaves the busy main road far behind it and heads down towards a village at the end of a cul-de-sac. "It was down here that they kept Napoleon's brother," Fitzroy nodded as they passed the signpost.

Donald frowned, "I beg your pardon."

"Yes you didn't know that one did you? Napoleon's brother lived here, he fell out with his brother over a woman, he was offered the kingdoms of Naples and Spain if he would give her up, but he wouldn't and we caught him trying to get to America. We put him here, let him buy a big house and put a man here to watch him day and night, he became the Prince of Grimley."

Donald drove down the road wildly, not knowing whether to believe that story but knowing that if anyone was coming the other way he would smash them off the road, "have you ever been here before?"

Fitzroy nodded, "Grim town? Yes but not too often. The people are strange here."

Donald looked at him and shook his head, "you know the way to the river though don't you?"

"Yes I knows it," Fitzroy grunted and checked his shot gun, he had been waiting a long time to use this on a man. "No one does that to my wife. That Londoner played us for us for couple of fools back there," he added.

"How do you mean?" Donald asked.

"Well he started that argument so that he could get away," Fitzroy replied.

Donald nodded, and for the first time ever I think he admired me, "do you still think I'm a Bolshevik?"

"I don't care about that anymore," Fitzroy replied, "I just want to get that bastard." They passed the church and the pub before Fitzroy pointed to a patch of grass, "park there! It's the closest we're going to get to the river; it's on foot from here."

Two villagers got out to stare at them and felt no shame in doing so, "that's one of them motor cars," one grunted.

"They must be from London," the other added, "that or another one of them bloody Bonapartes has come here."

"Do you like Londoners?" his friend grunted.

"No."

Of course neither had ever met a Londoner.

"I'm from Holt you stupid sods," Fitzroy replied, feeling bolder with the gun in his hands.

"What are you going to do with that?" The one man's face blanched.

"Shoot people," Fitzroy replied.

Both men draw back and Fitzroy smiled at the fear which whitened their alcohol reddened faces.

With that they headed off over the fields, into a dead land, "you shouldn't have said they may phone the police," Donald snapped.

"Do you really think that there is a phone here?!" Fitzroy laughed, "besides they don't likes people coming here from the outside." The land sank before them to a great lagoon which reminded Donald of some shell hammered corner of a battlefield. "Folk say that there use to be a brick works here.God knows what happened to it, if they took out too much soil or what, but now it is neither land nor river." It was now a dank, stagnant pit of rotting trees through which coots weaved in their frantic war paths.

"Will we catch them?" Donald asked.

"Yes if they are coming this way, we'll get them."

"What makes you so certain that they are coming this way?"

Fitzroy grinned, "people are lazy Mr Pembridge they won't want to fight against the Severn, they will just let her carry them downstream to Caerwrangon, besides that is the place they know, I doubt that London prat knows anything about Bridgnorth." He then paused and shook his head, "I mean you don't hit a woman like that do you?"

"I don't hit women at all," Donald lied.

Behind them another car pulled up behind Donald's, boxing it in so that they couldn't get out, the villagers scratched their heads, "looks like we're being invaded by men from Mars."

"Or London," the second added.

Kondrakov got out and looked at them with his soulless eyes, the two men looked away, "good day," the Russian greeted.

The villagers nodded and grunted something that people only from Grimley could have understood.

Kuperstein got out with a smile, "good day gentlemen what a charming village this is. Our friends just came here; do you know where they went?"

"Yes down there towards the pit," the other added.

Kondrakov was about to head off when the first man added, "you be careful mind, they've got a gun."

The Russian nodded, "well we'll have to take it away from them, won't we?"

The two headed off, Kuperstein's smile fading, "we should be careful, remember what they did to Howard."

"What he did," Kondrakov corrected he was only thinking of Donald.

Kuperstein nodded towards the lagoon, "that looks like the perfect place to hide two dead bodies."

"We have to kill them first,"

"So we are going to kill them?" Kuperstein asked.

Kondrakov shrugged, "why not?"

"But what will we get out of that?" Kuperstein replied.

"Revenge."

The German's eyebrows rose, "what for Howard? Are you joking? You always said that you felt like shooting him yourself!"

Kuperstein felt like he was being swept into a whirlpool of madness, he hadn't come from the same kind of hell as Kondrakov, there had been no war in Memel, well very little. His family had only fled in 1923 when the Lithuanians had invaded, showing two fingers to the world powers who had wanted to run the city themselves, most of the other Germans had stayed there though, his family had panicked and lost everything because of it. He looked over to Kondrakov, smoothing his hand down his pistol as if it was a penis, maybe it was time for him to say he would look after the car.

Donald and Fitzroy headed down to the river with Fitzroy leaning over, "what's going to happen if they escape?"

Donald shuddered, "I don't even want to think about that one, "He had a vision before him of the great palaces of Windsor and Balmoral collapsing into dust. "Maybe we will be ready then for your Mr Stuart to come back."

"Don't start that again!" Fitzroy laughed.

"How do you know that they haven't passed us already?" Donald asked looking towards the river.

Fitzroy shook his head, "that lazy London bastard ain't going to do any rowing, I can tell you that now, he'll let the Severn do all the work."

"After what he did to your wife he'll be in a panic for you not to catch him," Donald retorted.

Fitzroy nodded and venom returned to his eyes, "yes so he should be. I'll look upstream you look downstream, but what should I do if I find them?"

"Nothing follow them downstream until you meet me," Donald replied.

"Then what?"

"I think it's time to kill them, don't you?"

Fitzroy nodded and then headed up the river bank like a poacher.

The two headed off in opposite directions. Kondrakov's eyes settled on Fitzroy like an eagle, "you follow the other one, I'll get that one."

Kuperstein sighed, "OK," but both knew that Donald was the more dangerous of the two. Kondrakov felt like having an easy kill before he turned on the other, if Kuperstein wasn't dead before then of course. Kuperstein should turn back now; he knew that, the only time that he had fired a gun before was on the training ground.

Donald walked briskly at first and then started to run, he wasn't going to be the first Lord of Holt Castle to lose his charge, he wasn't going to let the British Empire collapse into chaos, the Pembridge family had been sliding down for centuries, all that was running through the tall man's mind as he ran, clawing the branches out of his way. Part of him wanted the baby to get away though, wanted it all to fall apart, the whole rotten baby killing system, but then he remembered the horrors that the reds had inflicted on Russia and imagined it coming here. He thought of killing me, of killing Matilda, of killing the baby, his mind was vivid with images of a dozen different futures.

Kuperstein ran after him, cursing every step, feeling like a school boy and Donald was a man, a killer, The German felt like he was running towards his own death. He tried to keep out of sight, but he needn't have bothered because the tall man never looked back once. Kuperstein reached a bend from where he could see a long way up the river and then slowed to a halt; Donald had disappeared, like a ghost. The German looked back, and was about to turn back when a silhouette launched itself out of the bushes at him, grabbing him by the throat and yanking him aside, the force nearly breaking his neck. Kuperstein felt a knee hammer up into his groin and he reeled over in pain, any fight going from him, and he looked up into Donald's face, deep into madness. Donald dragged him down like a large bird which had caught a mouse before he threw his head down into the river, "let me baptize you into hell! Now who the hell are you?" Kuperstein was still reeling with pain, but his lack of an answer earnt him another brutal kick in the side. "What's your name?"

"Kuperstein," he gurgled.

"A German?" Donald grinned, "you people never give up do you? Well at least it makes things easier; I have already killed plenty of Germans. Is that who you are working for?"

"No, no."

"Liar!" Donald snarled and kicked him viciously again.

"No, I'm an American."

"How much do you know?"

Donald drew back and let Kuperstein breath, the tall man's eyes almost seemed to shake like an Albino's, as he towered over him, Kuperstein's face quaked with terror, "we know it all, who the baby is, who you are and where you are keeping her."

Donald nodded, "is that so?" He then brought out his revolver and checked it.

"Hey, hey, hey you're not going to kill me are you? I haven't done anything to you."

Donald smiled as he watched his victim's eyes bulge white like a sheep about to be slaughtered; this gave him a sense of power, not just to defeat a rival, but to drive him into the dirt. "Give my regards to Buddha!" He snarled before squeezing the trigger, punching a hole in Kuperstein's head and splattering his brains into the mud, where it formed a dank cocktail which trickled down into the Severn. The tall man then sighed, he had better get some rocks to weigh him down and gut him before he dumped him into the river. He had done it once in Bucharest, the river that runs through that city is really too small to hide a corpse and the police found it a week later, of course he blamed the Germans and they blamed him. Donald though sighed, it was all time that he never had really, time he was wasting on a piece of dirt German who was working for the Yanks. He had cursed the Americans ever since 1919 when they strode into Versailles and turned a bloody victory into a defeat with their thirteen stupid points, and their President who belonged more in a Sunday school than a meeting of world leaders. Donald spat down on the young German's corpse, I guess it had to be done though, no sod it, he would see how Fitzroy was first.

Fitzroy stalked along the bank as if he was trying to flush out a fox, but the longer it took the more he was certain that the boat was not going to pass, "thieving Cockney bastard!" he grunted. Then he heard a gunshot, Donald! He must have cornered them downstream. Fitzroy went running off in the direction of shot when he saw a figure walk towards him, his head down. At first he thought it was Simmonds and almost took a shot at him until he saw it was a stranger and he ignored him, running towards him as if he was just an obstacle to pass. He was almost upon him when Kondrakov, unfurled himself, his coat thrown off his shoulders like a cape and his arm driving forwards like a man trap, hammering a knife deep into Fitzroy's throat. The Russian then watched without emotion the man sink, even though he was thousands of miles away he was the new Russia. The young man crouched down to watch Fitzroy writhe on the floor, trying to free himself of the blade stuck in his throat. Kondrakov shook his head with a knowing smile, Fitzroy would never have the strength to do that, his fingers touched on the blade's handle, but couldn't even grip it. "I'll let you keep that," the Russian smiled brushing the dirt from his coat and throwing it back over his shoulders, "something to remember me by."

Kondrakov's eyes were those of a NKVD torturer, there was a fascination there in watching the Englishman's suffering, only a few minutes before he had been a perfectly soundly working human being now he had malfunctioned. The Russians had almost risen into heaven itself, it had been a land of Saints whose faces glowed with holiness, but then they had sunk into satan's hell. Kondrakov rose to his feet. This had been his first kill, now he felt like a true man. He had seen plenty of dead bodies before, he remembered seeing fifty or so crows in a cornfield and he had run over to see a mound of corpses, stacked up like gigantic broken dolls, their eyes staring out into infinity. Maybe the reds had killed them, maybe the whites, probably the red s because their hate was the fiercest. He felt then that they had just been people and the men who had done that had been something else, now he was one of them. He had wanted to join the reds but he knew that he would not live long there; they would eventually turn on him, because he was the son of an aristocrat. He didn't know that he had just killed the last in a long line which had started with King John. Then he saw something in the dying man's eyes, for a moment he could read them, suddenly he jumped aside and turned as a shot plunged into the dirt beside him.

"You murdering bastard!" Like a phantom Donald ran towards Kondrakov, the Russian panicked and scrambled down towards the lagoon which could hide a thousand fugitives. Donald fired again but the young man vanished into the reeds. Donald's eyes then fell onto Fitzroy and he smiled, "war isn't like what you read in the books is it old chap?"

Fitzroy's lips mouthed, "kill me."

"You should be happy my friend you have died for the Hanoverian King, just like your sons did," Donald smiled before squeezing out the shot which ploughed Fitzroy's brains into the mud. He had no time to hide this corpse; he had to get the Russian!

Kondrakov froze as the shot thundered out and he clutched his revolver, he should turn and face Donald and shoot it out, but he knew that he would lose, Donald had come alive out of the war through sheer brutality, he wasn't just playing soldier, Donald was the real thing. Kondrakov scrambled up a bank and thanked God when he saw the cars.

The villagers were still sat there, one had taken to scratching his testicles as Kondrakov staggered back and frantically searched his pockets for the keys, "now there's a man in a hurry to leave."

"I don't know why we've had Princes live here," the other added.

"Maybe he owes someone some money," the first man laughed.

Kondrakov let out a happy yelp to find the keys and then opened the door before throwing himself at the starting handle, one of the villagers held up his hand and turned the handle for him, the car started and the villager reached forwards and tossed the handle onto the passenger seat before Kondrakov jammed the car into reverse and it sped off with the door still half open.

"Thank you for visiting our village," the first man mocked with a bow.

His face whitened as the car's breaks were slammed on and the Russian came back out with his gun, "I'm sorry," the yokel stammered.

Kondrakov smiled before firing at one of Donald's car wheels, blowing out it's tyre, the Russian's face then opened up in panic as Donald ran forwards, firing, sending the villagers scampering like rabbits. The bullet narrowly missed the Russian as he leapt back into the car. Donald tried to fire again but he was out of bullets. Kondrakov felt himself shake as he saw Donald run at him, his face blazing as if it was dowsed in petrol. The Russian stamped on the accelerator and looked back as he sent the car hurtling back up the road, past the church and the pub, where he span round and then sent the car forward . Donald nearly caught him there, he almost had his hand on the door handle but the car sped up the one way out of Grimley, and the place would never see it again.

"I reckon he must be sleeping with his wife," the first villager whispered, emerging from behind a hedge. His eyes then settled on Donald as he brought out his car keys, "that will do ye no good I am afraid."

"Why not?" Donald snarled.

The villager pointed to his wheel and Donald cursed to high heaven.

Chapter Eleven: The princess escapes.

Renda stood outside the pub fuming, his bags beside him, "there is no way out of this place! Can you believe this it's 1926, it might as well be 1026, these people are still living in the Stone Age."

I stood back in the pub doorway, "it's certainly different to London, that's for sure."

"I live in the middle of a desert," Renda continued, "but even there, there are buses and cars, and we are a thousand miles from shit!"

"We have to move soon," Matilda hissed.

"Don't you think I know that?" Renda looked as if he was on the brink of a heart attack.

"What happens if Donald comes back here first?" Matilda asked, "shouldn't we stay inside?"

"No," Renda replied, "you stay where you are, he will stop his car there walk towards you, do some shouting then I will shoot him in the back, simple."

"Hardly sporting," I replied, but I did like his plan, after all Donald had never seen him, so he wouldn't be ready for a shot in the back.

"Neither is baby killing," he retorted.

"That would make us like bait in a trap," Matilda asked.

I nodded, "yes it would."

"If I would have stayed," Matilda asked timidily, "do you think they would have done something to me?"

I was about to answer when Renda did that for me, "they would have killed you."

"Why?" She half sobbed.

Renda shrugged, "it's what I would do in their place, you know too much."

At that moment a car appeared on the hill and Liberato's hand sank into his pocket where his gun was.

"It's your car!" I cried.

"Let's not be celebrating yet," Renda barked, "we haven't seen who is driving it!"

Kondrakov's leg had been still shaking as he swerved out onto the main road almost hitting the road sign which said Tenbury one way and Worcester the other. He had looked in the rear view mirror still expecting to see Donald running after him with those abnormally long legs of his. Only now did his leg stop shaking as he saw Renda flag him over, angrily he bundled his baggage into the boot before rounding on Kondrakov, "where the hell have you been?"

"We went after Pembridge's car."

"And where the hell is Kuperstein?"

"I don't know," he lied.

"Well we can't wait for him, get in the car!" Renda shouted.

The landlord came out running, "where are you going?"

"Southampton," Renda replied.

"Southampton?" The landlord frowned.

"Yes it's a big city in the south of England,sorry that you have never heard of it," he then pulled out a five pound note and planted it in the landlord's hand, "there get yourself some American beer, the stuff you're serving tastes like piss."

I couldn't help but smile at that one, I got into the back of the car with Matilda and the baby and the car shot off towards Ombersley. The landlord watched us up the bank before shaking his head, "bloody Yank," he then looked down at the note, "that's pretty though.'

The Russian looked back at Holt Fleet, still expecting to see Donald come running after them, his eyes then fell on the baby, "is that the Princess?"

"No, it's some love child that I had with your momma," Renda replied, "now what happened back there?"

"I followed Fitzroy and he followed Donald, I heard a shot-"

Renda held up his hand and Kondrakov instantly fell silent, "you picked the easy one to follow, the yokel with a shot gun and you gave Kuperstein a man who is ten times as dangerous, a professional."

"Like us," Kondrakov muttered.

"Like me," Renda corrected. "No doubt he killed Kuperstein."

"I don't know," Kondrakov lied, "I just know that I had to get out of there in a hurry because Pembridge was after me."

Renda laughed, "you chicken shit coward, what happened to Fitzroy?"

"I killed him," Kondrakov admitted calmly.

"Fitzroy is dead?" Matilda exclaimed.

"Yes."

Renda's smile broadened, "you killed him deliberately didn't you Kondrakov? I mean it wasn't no self defence."

"He came at me," the Russian lied.

Renda shook his head slowly, "no he never, you killed him because you wanted to, you could have let him live, but you killed him just for kicks. If they catch you you'll hang for that my friend."

Kondrakov felt a chill run through him, "they have to catch me first."

"You talk like one mean ass kicker, only I ain't convinced, a real hard man would have killed both of them. I always knew that you were the wild one, maybe you will kill me one day," Renda laughed, "or at least try. You've just made things worse now, there will be hundreds of police after us now, this isn't Russia you know, you can't just kill people and blame foreign agents."

"Yes, but this time it was foreign agents," Kondrakov smiled.

Renda leant back in his chair and admired the countryside, "well I have my alibi, that nosey bastard of a landlord back there, you will hang alone." His eyes then returned to the countryside as if he never had a care in the world, "isn't it amazing how they can farm with such little fields? Back home our fields go on forever." The car stopped at the crossroads at Ombersley, Kondrakov was about to take the car right when Renda pulled his hand the other way, "no left."

"But Southampton is south."

"Who said that we were going to Southampton?" Renda replied.

"You did."

"That's just what I told that idiot back there, head to Stourport," Renda replied calmly.

"Do you know where we're going?" I asked.

"Don't you think I had enough time back there to plan our escape? I know the roads well enough, I do not need a map," Renda replied.

We headed north, past the Bishop of Worcester's castle, which was an old ramshackle before plunging down a steep bank towards Stourport, a Victorian place which had grown up around the spot where the canal from Birmingham entered the Severn, money had built a town out of nothing. "We should stop here and get some food," Matilda asked.

"At the next place," Renda replied and then pulled out one of those small red guidebooks, "the next place it says is Bewdley. Ah it's a shame that we aren't living centuries ago because it says here that it use to be a free town."

"What is that?" Matilda asked.

"A place where a fugitive from the law could go and the King's men would not touch him."

"I can see Donald respecting that," I grunted.

The car carried on and left the Victorian canal town behind it. Bewdley was a pretty enough place, too pretty to accept the canal going through it,and that is why Stourport had been built. Renda glanced out of the car before turning to Kondrakov, "carry on."

"But you promised," Matilda protested.

"I promised," Renda replied,"nothing. This place is still too close; I want to be out of this county before we go shopping."

The darkness of the Wyre Forest closed around us, but it still looked ravaged after nearly being near completely cut down during the war when the country had almost run out of wood. The only old trees that still stood were those no good for timber, the rest were all saplings of youthful green. The dears too had been hunted mercilessly so that only a few now remained and they kept in the shadows like distant ghosts. Once the forest had swamped the whole river valley, surrounding Worcester itself, giving the city her name, but over the centuries it had been hacked back to this miserable pocket.

Matilda looked at Renda as he admired the scenery, "do you like England Mr Renda?"

Renda smiled broadly, "we Americans do not think as you do, like your King who went to France and built an alliance with them simply because he liked to party there. It is not a case of liking or not liking England, we are competitors. When two horses fight over a mare they do not stop to wonder if they like each other. No they come at each other with teeth and hooves."

We followed the river north to where great cliffs rose, pock marked with caves, on top of those cliffs the town of Bridgnorth stood. It had held out valiantly for the king during the civil war and when the republicans had finally taken it they had burnt it to the ground and sent the people out to live in the fields. One wall of the old castle was all that was left of the original town, and it was leaning over precariously. Renda's eyes followed the cable car which climbed up the cliff, "you know this town was going to be the German's HQ if they invaded England."

"I have never heard of such a thing," I grumbled.

Renda smiled, "I have seen the maps and their lines of communication lead to here."

"Why don't we stop here then?" Matilda asked, "we're out of Worcestershire now."

Renda's eyes followed the cable car as it climbed up the cliff, "no, it looks like the kind of place that is easy to go into but not so easy to come out of, we will stop at the next place."

"We will have to," Matilda argued, "it is getting late now."

"Nonsense it is only just three," Renda smiled.

The road should have carried onto Shrewsbury, the county town of Shropshire but they turned off up a narrower road, and drove half an hour until they saw a black and white sign which said: 'Newport.'

"I thought that was in Monmouthshire," Matilda frowned.

Renda grinned, "it is, I went there once."

"Why?"

"Trying to cause trouble, you know, Monmouthshire should be in Wales, Wales should be free, but we could find no takers," Renda moaned.

"You don't surprise me," I muttered.

"The Welsh remind me of the type of negro we have back home, I mean the blacks who are still loyal to us even though we treat them like dirt, I mean we crap all over them but they still call themselves American and go off and fight in our wars." Renda smiled, "some people don't want to be free. The thing about Newport though is that it is a port, at the mouth of the river Usk, here there is not even a river, just fields."

"Maybe there was a river here once," Kondrakov replied.

"What is that supposed to mean?" Renda replied.

"Like places with castle in the name, but the castle has long gone."

"That's castles," Renda retorted, "castles can be destroyed, how can you get rid of a river?"

"There was a great Hungarian king once who moved a river," Kondrakov replied.

"No great Humgarian king has ever been here, look around, it's a butt hole of a place, don't get all mystic and Russian with me now," Renda mocked.

Newport was a typical Shropshire market town, once it had had some glory days when money had flowed in, but those days were long gone, and the legacy only lay in some buildings that were obviously too grand for such a place. Kondrakov parked the car on the main street and got out to open the door for Matilda. Renda got out and took the door from him, "now little lady you come with me and tell me what you need."

I watched Renda barge Matilda into a shop and smiled, at least I felt safe now, with him there, there was a brutishness about him, it was like walking at night with a huge, vicious dog at your side, but then you never knew when the dog might turn on you, my eyes glanced around the town, "it looks like nothing has ever happened here for a long time."

"Let's try to keep it that way," Kondrakov replied, "I'm going to stretch my legs."

I watched as Kondrakov strode off towards the church then I glanced at Renda, Matilda and the baby, I should have kept my eye on them, but instead I was more interested in where the Russian was going. Kondrakov's head sank as he neared the church like a naughty urchin returning home. He paused and looked over it before tilting open the church door then breathing in the musk. There was none of the fragrances of a Russian church but it still bore the smell of centuries. Across his country people were burning churches down now, setting light to places where they had been baptized, married and seen their kin buried. In a way he could understand it, it was like freeing yourself from the past. He looked back into his own church, where he had been an altar boy, he remembered counting the people who would take communion for the priest every week, no doubt that place had gone now and the priest was either in a gulag or dead. The Russian was about to go back out when he saw something and slowly edged towards it, leaving the door open behind him.At first he had thought that he had imagined it, but in a corner, with a prayer cushion before it was an Orthodox icon, and it was not just the church's saint but his! Saint Nicholas!It was not the best artwork, the Serbian soldier had painted it had been invalided here during the war, and before he had left to go home he gave it to the church where he had prayed so much. The eyes caught Kondrakov and they looked at him with anger and disappointment and fear. The altar boy walked slowly forwards as I edged through the open doorway behind him. Then I watched as a killer brought his lips to kiss those of a saint. Then he drew back and crossed himself, the first man to have done so since that Serbian soldier, and the place seemed to change as if he had sprinkled some magic there, or maybe it was my imagination. I drew back, wanting to dismiss it as papist nonsense but I couldn't, I had felt something myself.

I walked back to the car before the Russian could see me, my eyes met Renda as he emerged from a ladies clothes shop, "where's Kondrakov?"

I nodded back to the church, "praying."

Renda sighed,"oh he's one of them is he?"

"What do you mean?" I asked.

"Like the Italians back home, they gun someone down in Chicago or wherever and then head straight to church, confess it all to the almighty, get forgiven for it and then they are ready for action again."

"What do you do then?" I asked.

"Look at that flag down there," he pointed to a rather withered Union flag, "the crosses of St George, St Andrew and St Patrick. The Scandinavians only have one cross on their flags, you have three! How that's for being God fearing? My flag has no room for any kind of cross; it has stars and thirteen stripes, the number of a witch's covenant."

"Now you are beginning to sound mystical," I laughed.

Renda nodded and then drew out his wallet and produced a dollar bill, "look at this note, where is the Christianity there? Look at the pyramid with an eye in it, I mean what the hell is all that meant to mean? It is there before you, but the world never sees it." Renda returned the note to his wallet, "I am an American; that is what I do."

Kondrakov came out of the church and headed back to the car, Renda mocked him, "so you have said all your *kyrie eleisons* now and swung your incense have you? Can we go now?"

Kondrakov looked at him, evil creeping into the coldness and for the first time Renda felt a shot of fear.

The villagers helped Donald change the wheel, part out of fear, part out of a wish to see the back of this strange figure. "It was a funny thing to do to shoot a car," the first man grumbled.

"They do funny things Londoners do," the second noted.

"He didn't want him going after him," the first man concluded.

"'Has he been riding your wife?" The second man asked.

"No! I am not married," Donald replied, the fight gone from him, there was no point in being in a hurry now, they were a long way away, he thought about going back and hiding the bodies, but it was hardly worth it, if the bodies were found he'd blame the Americans, besides one phone call from the palace and nothing else would be said of it. He thought about phoning the police himself, but then the villagers would do that when they found the bodies. Only now did he think of the young, handsome man who he had killed, and he didn't know what had come over him, he had been a monster, it hardly seemed like him now. He should get away from this life, but what else would he do? He had no money, he had to work.

The villagers put the wheel on and Donald hurriedly looked into his wallet before pulling out a couple of notes, "there we are Sir?" The two looked up lie expectant puppies.

Donald handed them the notes, "thank you," he grunted.

The villagers grabbed the notes and then looked at him, "one more thing Sir."

"What is it?"

"Never come to Grimley again."

Donald's face flashed with anger then he looked at them and smiled, maybe they were right, "no I don't think I will, goodbye."

He was going to drive back to Holt, but what was the point? When he got to the main road he nearly swung right but instead he turned left towards Worcester. There was only one man in Worcestershire who could possibly know where they were going, for the first time it all seemed rather stupid, all the old traditions, calling the city by different names, not straying outside the county. He drove down into the city, the cripples were heading home now, if they had a home, dusk swept over the city, the cathedral was just an unlit silhouette now. He drove past the racecourse and then his eyes settled on the twinkling lights of the prison, even they had a home. He parked in front of it and sighed before checking his gun once more before heading out.

As he entered the hospital a nurse instantly rushed towards him, "Sir, can I help you?"

"The man who came in here with a gunshot wound to his leg, where is he?"

"It is not visiting hours."

Donald was not in the mood for this, "I didn't ask that, where is he? I am from the Police."

The nurse's face then changed, she would never know how close she came to getting a slap that night as she showed Donald down the corridors, into the ward where Defford lay, Donald then turned to the nurse and smiled sweetly, "thank you sister."

Donald was now weary and he seemed to drag his feet into where Defford was asleep, he drew the curtains around them before them and clamped his hand over Defford's mouth. The American's eyes then opened to meet the face he had just seen in his nightmare and they sweated fear, he thought about biting the hand before he saw his revolver creep up like a snake. "Remember me Mr Defford? Now I am going to take my hand away and you are not going to scream, are we agreed?"

Defford nodded and the hand slowly drew back, "what do you want?"

"Your friends have left," Donald replied.

"Don't you think that you have a hell of a nerve coming here?"

"They have the baby and are heading for the coast," Donald guessed.

"Then what are you doing here?" Defford sneered.

Donald ignored him, "so you are all alone now, apart from one of your young colleagues who I killed, he is bleeding his brains out into the river at Grimley. Apparently Napoleon's brother use to live there, did you know that? You can join him if you like unless you tell me what you know."

Defford frowned, "what do you mean?"

"Where are they going to? How are they going to get to America?" Donald hissed.

Defford looked up at him, "I don't know."

Donald smacked the gun into his cheek, "do you want me to finish the job?"

Derfford's hand clawed at the bed, "I don't know I tell you!"

"You know I will use this don't you?" Donald snarled.

"Yes."

"Then tell me, where are they?"

Defford's eyes bore the expression that he didn't care anymore, "do you think my boss tells me every detail of his plans? I only know what I have to know. I know he has a boat somewhere, but I don't know where. If I knew I would tell you, but I don't!"

Donald felt like shooting him anyway but instead he just drew back, he believed him, the gun lowered, "alright, I hope you get well soon, and I am sorry."

"Thank you," Defford replied through gritted teeth then breathed a deep sigh of relief; the war was over for him now at least.

Donald walked out through the ward a beaten man and drifted out of the hospital, he went towards his car but he didn't know where he was going, nowhere now. He was about to cross the road when a hand fell on his shoulder, "Mr Pembridge?" A stocky bull dog of a man stood behind him.

"Yes."

"I know where they are going."

"Who?"

"The Americans, with your baby, I know where they are going."

"Who are you?" There was something familiar about the man, as if he had seen him before somewhere.

"Winston Churchill."

"But you were in the government."

"That's a lifetime away now," he smiled. "Come on we will take my car."

They got into the car which was already running and drove off, the driver was a black man and Donald's eyes fell on him for a moment. The tall man's eyes then retuned to Churchill, he was known as the man who had dreamt up the Gallipoli fiasco, Donald never knew that he had also dreamt up the tank. He had cursed him many times because of his brother's death, "how do you know about all this?"

Churchill chuckled, "you people who work for the palace think that you know everything and that we in the government are stupid, well we got the better of you last time it came to a fight. We know who you are Mr Pembridge, we know about Holt Castle and Dunstall Castle as well for that matter. We know about the princess who was born twice, one of nature's little accidents."

"So what are you going to do about it?"

"You should trust us more; we are all on the same side. We have to stop them getting to that boat, once they get to the high seas they will be gone and the Yankees will use that baby against us." His eyes then fell on the driver, "drive!"

The darkening city sped past them as they headed north towards Kidderminster, the roads were empty so they could move fast, as soon as the last light faded from Worcester they headed into complete blackness, they sped through Ombersley with such a gust to nearly knock a passerby over. "But why? Why are the Americans doing this?"

Churchill smiled, "the idiots in Whitehall don't get it, they still live in the times of Prussia and cavalry charges, even after all that carnage. They think of enemies like the French and Germans, the people over the channel we don't like very much, but they basically play by the rules. They don't know what the Americans are like. They are ruthless and they play to win! They want to finish us and our empire, do you have a pistol?"

"Yes," Donald nodded.

"Good, because you will need it," Churchill replied.

Donald nodded, "yes I already bagged one."

"Did you? Oh good show," with that he got himself a small bottle of whisky and a even smaller glass and poured himself one, "best have some as well, it is a long way to Flintshire."

"Is that where we are going?"

Churchill nodded, "yes Uncle Sam doesn't like to use big ports like Liverpool or Holyhead; he likes places where people don't see him. Uncle Sam," Churchill paused and his eyes glinted, "is the kind of bastard uncle who use to touch your sister up a bit."

Donald laughed, "yes do you think we'll make it? I mean they must be four hours ahead us?"

"Kingsley here is a very good driver, besides if we don't get them here, we'll torpedo them at sea."

"You can do that?"

Churchill grinned, "my dear man, I have contacts everywhere, one phone call to the admiralty and the biggest navy in the world will send the good ship Robert E. Lee to the bottom of the sea!"

Chapter Twelve: The Last Lord of Holt Castle.

We headed through Chester passing through one of the gateways in it's city wall and past the rather humble cathedral, my eyes glimpsed the streets where lines of shops stood on top of other shops, it was unlike any other city in Britain. Then we drove up the river Dee, like a black carpet which lead into Flintshire and Wales. It was dark now and the moonlight danced on the estuary. Matilda felt pangs in her heart, she was leaving her country and would no doubt never see England again. She had been poor all her life, but still she would miss it. Flint itself was a scrawny little town but it's castle looked as if it had been built to withstand an attack by giants. This was where the English had always lived down by the sea, in the hills, overlooking the town was where the Welsh lived, amidst the remnants of Offa's Dyke, like wolves watching a pack of dogs. We drove through the town, heading up a coast of old ships, rusting into the sea, each hulk resembled some old monster, silhouetted against the moon. "What is this place?" I gasped.

"The pirate coast," Renda smiled, "if you are a passenger you go to Liverpool, if you are a bandit you come here."
"Can you sail to Ireland from here?" Matilda asked.

"You can sail to anywhere from here," Renda smiled, "these people would take you to Antartica if the price is right, no passport needed, no questions asked."

The road was straight and looked as if it would go on forever, and the Russian almost seemed to be dozing off at the wheel.

"Down there!" Renda suddenly ordered.

"Down there?" Kondrakov repeated.

"Yes! Down there!" We veered off and headed down a dirt track, half sliding down it before coming to rest before an old fishing boat.

"Are we going in that?" Matilda asked.

"What did you expect Douglas Fairbank's yacht?" Renda smirked.

"Well it would have been nice," I replied.

Kondrakov parked up the car and turned the headlamps off, he then staggered out, nursing his back, he looked at the boat, it reminded him of the one his family had escaped Russia in, every inch crowded with duchesses and dukes. He had watched two women he recognized as being at the top of Petrograd society before the war fight like alley cats for the last place, the boat went without them both, and they were left to the mercy of the Soviets, no doubt both had been raped as soon as they had got there.

I looked back at the Welsh hills and Renda smiled, "I can read your mind Mr Simmonds."

"Really?"

"Yes you have some crazy idea of hiding up in those hills, well I can tell you they would find you, you can't hide anywhere now, not on this island, the place is just too small;the only people who disappear here are dead. If you want to see Britain again come back in another twenty years," Renda smiled, "we will be running the place by then."

"I hope all Americans aren't like that," Matilda sighed.

"Yes it does get to you after a while doesn't it?" I replied, and wondered if I hadn't made a huge mistake, then I looked back at the baby and knew that I hadn't.

Renda pulled out his pistol before cautiously walking up the gang plank, in a military way which looked fake to me because I knew that he had never been a real soldier, only a butcher who had shot unarmed natives. He looked back at us, "what the hell is this Marie Celeste?"

"Not quite," a rifle emerged from the shadows and rested next to Renda's head, behind it a tall mixed race man stood. For a moment there was a tense silence and Kondrakov's hand drew towards his own pistol. The stranger then stepped forwards and looked over Renda's face, he was the ship's captain, and had been an alcohol smuggler between Jamaica and Miami when Renda had met him. He would do anything for money, greedy people were always easier to predict that patriots. Slowly the rifle lowered, "well you took your time."

Kondrakov breathed a sigh of relief, he could have killed the man, but he wasn't a good enough shot not to kill his boss as well.

"Get ready to sail," Renda replied.

"Nothing would make me happier, I have been waiting six months for this, but we will have to wait until the morning," the Captain moaned.

"What the hell for?"

"There is a storm in the Irish Sea."

Renda looked out into the darkness, "looks calm enough to me."

"It is further west, off Anglesey."

Renda nodded, "alright, but if the coppers come we will have to leave before that, storm or no storm."

The Captain then nodded towards us as I helped Matilda on board, her arms gripping the baby, "who are they?"

"Our passengers; that is Charlie Simmonds and this is Matilda," Renda paused, "I'm sorry I don't know your surname."

"Coker," she replied.

"Coker?" Renda frowned, "sounds like some black guy who plays the trumpet; we shall have to change that."

"And what of the baby?" Calloway nodded towards her.

"The baby? The baby is the prize, why we have spent six months searching England," Renda announced.

"I could have found you a load of babies back home, I could have made you some if you'd had wanted," Calloway quipped.

"Not like this one," Renda replied.

"She don't look much to me," the captain shrugged,

"And do you have a name?" I asked.

"Calloway," he replied.

"Well Mr Calloway," I started.

"Captain," he cut in.

"What?"

"Captain Calloway, this boat might not be the Lusitania and I might be a bit darker than an Italian, but I am still a captain," he snapped.

I bowed slightly, "yes of course."

"English are you?" Calloway grunted.

"Yes."

"My mother always use to say that my father was English, but other times she said that he was French."

I smiled, "well let's hope it's the former."

Calloway nodded, "one thing's for sure I hope he wasn't Welsh, I am sick of this place now." He looked along the dark hills and cursed them.

"Have you seen much of Wales?" I seemed to spend a lot of time those days defending Wales and the Welsh, I don't know why I even cared, since I don't have even one drop of Welsh blood.

"Just along this coast, back into Flint really and what a crap hole that is," he grumbled.

"Actually there are some very beautiful places in Wales," I argued.

"No there ain't," Calloway replied, "it's all crap I can see that from here."

I shrugged, well at least I had tried.

"Where are the other two?" Calloway asked.

"One is in hospital with a gunshot wound, the other is dead," Renda replied, matter of factly.

"Which one is in the hospital?" Calloway asked.

"Howard."

"Good that will teach him a lesson, who is dead?"

"Kuperstein," Renda replied.

"Good," Calloway smiled, "he was a cocky one; well he ain't so cocky now."

Kondrakov's face flinched, he had felt like he was falling in love with Kuperstein at one stage, but now he felt nothing, not even anger at Calloway, what kind of a person was he, why didn't he have the same set of emotions as other people had?

"Guess not," Renda agreed.

Calloway's eyes were fixed in the silhouetted hills, "six months in this place alone, it's enough to send you crazy," then he remembered that he hadn't been totally alone, "what do you plan to do with the car?"

Renda smiled, he had never thought of that, of course they couldn't take it with them, "I guess we'll just leave it here."

"Is the bill of sale and all the documents of ownership inside?" Calloway asked.

Renda looked back at Kondrakov who nodded, "yes it's all in the glove compartment."

"I was wondering if I couldn't give it to a young lady I knew down in Flint," Calloway rubbed his palms together; he wasn't use to asking for things off people, because he usually didn't get them, and because of that he usually just took them.

"It couldn't have been that bad here then," Renda smiled.

"You haven't seen her," Calloway muttered.

Renda looked at the car, it was a beauty, not as flash as Donald's but then they weren't trying to draw attention to themselves, but what could they do with it? The embassy wouldn't want it because they didn't know about any of this and it would simply lead the police to them. It was better Calloway's woman had it, "yes sure you can have it."

""I'll drive it down there," Calloway replied.

"No I don't want you getting distracted down there," Renda replied.

"You haven't seen her," Calloway repeated.

Kondrakov stepped forwards, "I'll go, give me the address."

"How will he find it?" Matilda asked.

"There can't be that many streets in Flint," Renda laughed, "it looked like a right flea bag of a town when we drove through it."

"It is right opposite the castle," Calloway added and then went into his cabin to write down the address and a short note.

"But why bother?" I asked.

"it is better that the car isn't here, " Renda explained, "if someone has followed us here then it might throw them off, let them go house to house in Flint first. I reckon they will hassle his lady a bit, but after she has told them everything they will leave her alone, with the car. Now it isn't important what they know, not now that we have won."

Kondrakov's eyes sank into his boss's, "just don't leave without me."

"I wouldn't dream of it, besides you heard Calloway, there's a storm out there," Renda replied, but there was something devious in his eyes.

"I'll go with you," I offered.

Kondrakov felt better about that, he knew Renda wanted me to go with them. Calloway emerged with his scrap of paper, his last note to his lover and he handed it to the Russian, Kondrakov had never liked him, mainly because with his brown skin he had reminded him of a Gypsy, but also there was nothing fine or elegant about the man.

"The address is on there," Calloway then looked down, "my lips have kissed some beautiful women, some very beautiful woman, as a sailor you meet a lot, but this is not Marseille or Manila, and well, you have to make the best with what is offered."

Kondrakov nodded as he took the address, "I'll find it." He then looked at me before we headed back down the gang plank.

"What will you do if the police come before they are back?" Matilda whispered to Renda.

"Well leave of course," he replied as if it had been the most stupid question that he had ever heard.

Calloway then pulled out his telescope.

"What are you doing?" Renda frowned.

"Just making sure that those bastards actually go there," he would follow our headlamps, not hard to do in a sea of black.

I sat beside Kondrakov and looked at him warily as we drove into the Flintshire darkness before the Russian's dead eyes turned to me, "what is it? Why are you satring at me?"

"Why did you kill Fitzroy?"

Kondrakov looked at me like a disturbed lion, "it was the heat of battle you know?"

"No it wasn't."

Kondrakov nodded, "no it wasn't."

"So why did you do it for?"

The Russian shook his head, "I hardly know myself now, I have seen so many people killed in my life, it seemed like my turn to do a bit, you know."

"Actually I don't," I confessed.

"Besides he seemed so helpless, an easy kill, that's why I went after him, I had to makesure my first time didn't go wrong," Kondrakov spoke blandly as if it was nothing. "Like a youing man sleeping with a prostitute to lose his virginity I guess."

"And your friend bought it going after Donald?" I asked.

He nodded and smiled, "it's better that he bought it than me."

I looked back towards the boat, "do you think that he will wait for us?"

Kondrakov nodded, "if there is no storm he will."

"What if there is?" I asked.

"Then he won't."

"If they catch you, you'll hang," I reminded him.

He nodded, death at least would be a release, a release from his own madness and the past, "no they will not risk any of this coming out, we will both be dead in a ditch somewhere." The darkness passed and his eyes remained fixed in front, "now I have a question for you Mr Simmonds, why did you want to come with me?" That was met with silence, before he added, "you don't think that I will take the car to her do you?"

I paused, "no you would have taken the car to her, then go inside her house and kill her."

Kondrakov's eyebrows rose but he never denied it, "why ever do you say that?"

"You're a killer now, you've got a taste for it, it's a craving."

Kondrakov smiled, "so you are here to save the fair Welsh damsel, how very noble of you."

"This is going to be a long walk back," I noted.

"Are you afraid of the walk or of me?"

"Both," I replied.

The castle had been built as part of Edward I's ring of iron encircling North Wales, and the Welsh ahd attacked it many times and had been defeated many times, it had taken Cromwell to take the castle from the King and he had turned it into a ruin. Still it was a tribute to the Welsh that a few thousand mountain boys had needed such a citadel like this to keep them out.

We drove down one street then another until we found the right one, outside a rundown Victorian terrace we drew up and I got out to knock the door. Around us Flint was asleep, it was a poor place even by Welsh standards, God only knew what they did for work out here.

"Maybe we should shove the letter and keys through the letter box and just go," Kondrakov hissed.

"We will do if the silly cow don't get up in a minute," I replied.

The neighbour's curtains twitched before her's , it was only a glimpse of the car that lead her to open the door, and our eyes met a brutish looking woman with three chins who had never been pretty, "what do you want?"

Kondrakov handed the keys over and Calloway's letter.

"I can't read," she grunted without a hint of shame.

"It's from Calloway," Kondrakov replied, "he's leaving."

"Is he now the bastard?!" She roared loud enough for the neighbours to hear, but she didn't care what they thought anymore, "well it's a good job I didn't let him get me pregnant then isn't it?!"

I shook my head; she looked well past that age, "he has left you a present."

"What?"

"This car," I replied.

The woman staggered back, almost collapsing into her own front room, "it isn't stolen is it?"

"The documents for it are in the glove compartment, the bill of sale and all that," Kondrakov added, "he cannot take it back to America with him."

"I didn't even know he had a car," the woman replied.

"No ," I stepped back, "it has been with us in London."

"London," she gasped like the idiots at Holt Fleet had.

I then nodded, "good night my lady."

As we walked off the woman slowly emerged from her house to gaze with wonder at it. It was like the golden carriage from the fairytales her grandmother had read to her. She would be the only person in Flint to have a car! And what a car! She would die before she sold it! The curtains began to twitch around her, curtains of the people who had stopped her going to church, who had called her a whore, she nodded, "this is mine!" She declared, "this is my motor car!"

Flint sank into darkness again as the two outsiders walked out of it, the short ride down would be a long walk back along the elephant's graveyard of rusting giants, "who do you think they all belong to?" I asked to break the silence, "I mean it seems daft to have a ship like that and then just let it rust."

Kondrakov nodded, "must be dirty money then."

We past one that towered over us like a cathedral and my eyes fell on the Russian again, "so the baby will be safe with Renda?"

Kondrakov gave a sinister smile, "if I say no, what are you going to do about it?"

"I might surprise you," I replied.

The Russian ignored that, "it's too late to ask that now. I mean whatever you say he isn't going to give you back the baby now, after all that we have been through. I mean this has been some operation. Look at that car back there, it cost a small fortune and we've just given it to some Welsh tart."

"But the baby will be OK?" I asked again.

"Yes of course, she is our trump card," Kondrakov replied.

I nodded, "yes I have heard that expression a few times."

"Well it's true, now the British prime minster can say nothing when he talks to the Americans, maybe he doesn't know himself but whenever he talks to us, if he isn't 100% compliant he will be getting a phone call off the palace. The British own the patent on pnemutaic tyres; we have to pay every time we make one, because some Scottish asshole invented it; that is the first thing that will go."

"What if our PM says no?" I asked.

"Then we will say: 'fuck you we have your princess!' Then we will say that she actually is the older twin and should be queen and no one can prove nothing between identical twins.I bet in Washington they are already writing up a long list of demands."

"What have I done?" I murmured, "I betrayed my country."

Kondrakov smiled, "not like me then, my country betrayed me. What else could you have done? They had a gun to a baby's head? Besides we all sell out everyday you might as well be on the winning side."

The Russian almost seemed human now, I looked over to the distant lights of Birkenhead, "so you're American now are you?"

"No I am still Russian, but I can't go back home, they are killing people for fun."

"Sounds like your kind of place," I quipped.

"My family fought for the whites, my father was burnt alive by the Bolsheviks, in front of the whole village where he had once been lord, I can never go back," he lamented.

I began to see what had killed his soul and had given death to his eyes, "but the Americans can't beat us, we have the greatest empire on earth."

"They already kicked you out of Ireland didn't they?, If they can do that in a place where you had been for centuries how hard will it be to get you out of India?" Kondrakov marveled at the intrigues of his new country."Of course the Germans built the groups up in Ireland, but we continued their work after the war, and we are still funding people in the North; which will be an open wound for you for years to come."

I was getting to feel angry, angry and ashamed, but why should I be? What did I owe them? What had the British Empire ever done for me, save put my life in danger for four years? Only luck had saved me. "What will they really do with us, I mean in America?"

Kondrakov looked at me and laughed, "you worry about that? I should worry about that! They need you to back up their whole story, who will ever listen to me and Renda? No they need English accents, people who can be traced back to wherever you come from, real people."

"I don't think I can stop being English though," I admitted.

 The Russian smiled, "then when you get your house in America buy an old map of Yorkshire, or wherever you are from and put it on the wall, that's what everyone else does. There are German Americans, they are Germans but when the war comes they go off and kill their brothers, just as keenly as the others." He then looked up at the hills, "you know back home those woods would be filled with wolves and bears, I know that here there is nothing here bigger than foxes but still you feel afraid, even with a gun in your pocket."

That sent a chill through me; Kondrakov could kill me anytime he wanted I was unarmed.

Calloway followed us through the telescope or thought he did, "can you see anything?" Renda asked.

"Only the night," the sailor replied.

"No one's out there?" Renda urged.

"Oh there's always someone out there in the night, you can't see them but they are always there," Calloway then walked back into the cabin.

Renda shook his head, "asshole."

Matilda looked at Renda, never had she heard so much bad language, her mother would stick a bar of soap in his mouth to wash it out.Only now did she leave the baby alone, sleeping in the cabin. As she entered the cabin her eyes fell on her and she smiled, then she looked up at the sailor, "where are you from Captain Calloway?"

The sailor smiled, "all over the place Mam, when I was a kid we had to keep moving."
"Why?"

"My mother was white and you can see my colour," he smiled sadly, "as soon as I was old enough I took to the seas, there ain't no colour out here."

It was an empty road from Worcester to Flintshire, no car lights passed them, Market Drayton looked as if it had been abandoned for years, a ghost town lost in the black. Churchill had a confidence about him, he sat there was an amused smile on his face, "Americans are not like Europeans, we say we like people or not like them to their face, but with Americans you never know what is inside here," he tapped his forehead. "We Europeans tore ourselves apart all because of what some Serbian terrorist did one day."

"What could we have done?" Donald protested, "there were alliances, treaties had been signed."

"Treaties?" Churchill scoffed, "that is the old world. In the new world you sign what you like, like a bankrupt signing a cheque. That is the Bolshevik way, that is the Facist way, and that is the American way, sit on the sidelines, sell arms to both sides and then go in on the winning side. America is never happier than when two other countries are destroying themselves."

The driver looked back, "which way now boss?"

"Take the left road Kingsley we are entering Wales, have you ever been there before?"

"No Sir, I ain't, but then there's a lot of places that I ain't been," the black man replied.

Donald's eyes then narrowed, "where is he from?"

"Jamaica," Churchill replied.

Donald nodded, "you don't meet many black people in England."

"There are a lot of black Americans here now, oh they love it here," Churchill smiled, "they can live like people here, over there they are hated from the moment they are born until the day they die and never get a moment of peace in between." Churchill's drawl captivated him; how he elongated words you never expected to be stretched out.

"Where are we going?" Donald asked as they passed Connah's Quay and entered the ancient land of Wales.

"The Americans have a boat here, it's only a fishing boat but it will take them over the Atlantic, we have been lucky that there is a storm in the Irish Sea, otherwise they would be gone already."

"How do you know this?"

"I have heard the shipping report," he replied simply. He then pulled out his revolver, this was no office politician, Churchill had used that gun before now, he had been a fugitive in the Boer war; he had had a price on his head.

"How did you know about Holt Castle? I mean it has been a secret for centuries," Donald replied.

"And we have known about it for centuries too," Churchill chuckled.As the car sped along the Flintshire coast Churchill gave the kind of speech he did in parliament, or on the lecture circuit, or to a couple of drunks in pub. "The Americans have the dream of Alexander, of Napoleon, the dream on conquering the world!" They passed Flint's mighty castle and Churchill's eyes crossed it, "see that place? That is the old way of taking over a country, castles ands armies. Now you have to be more subtle, now is the time of the thief."

The road before them was a horizon less tunnel of black, the moon had hidden itself behind the blackest rainclouds, retreating armies from the storm, "pull in here," Churchill coughed.

"What here boss?"

"Yes Kingsley, in there."

 The black man steered down the muddy track, half way down Churchill leant over and turned the headlamps off, the black man looked up at him with fear, "now I can sees where I'm going."
"Let's try not to announce our visit, let's keep it a secret," Churchill smiled. Their eyes settled on the boat, it looked deserted but both men knew better, they could sense there was someone inside hiding."Now stop here," Churchill hissed. Kingsley applied the brakes and the car slowly slid to a halt, Churchill then opened the door and stepped outside and then gave any assassin a good target to aim at, he then looked back at Donald, "so are you coming?"

Donadl hastily checked his pistol, "yes I'm ready."

Churchill then strode down the road like a bulldog, Kingsley never offered to go and no one asked him, Donald glanced back and watched him sink beneath the steering wheel. Churchill brandished the gun like it was a tankard of ale, "it's been a long time since I held one of these in my hand."

"Wish I could ay the same," Donald smiled.

Churchill chuckled, "you got one of them in the leg didn't you?"

"Yes," Donald nodded.

"He was lucky," Churchill grunted, "I would have killed him."

As they walked towards the boat Donald looked up it's battered side, "are they really going to America in that?"

Churchill smiled, "what did you expect ? A yacht with the stars and stripes flying from it's a stern and a black man playing the banjo? Britannia still rules the waves; we'd sink that in an eyebat."

The two crept forwards, "are you sure that that is the right boat, there's nobody there?" Donald whispered, but he knew that was not the case.

"They're in there alright, I can smell the stench of rat," Churchill snarled, he stepped forwards and his upper lip stiffened, "come out, come out ratty," slowly his finger settled on the trigger. Donald looked at him in wonderment, after Gallipoli he had seemed like an idiot, but there was not a hint of fear in his face now.

"There's nobody here," Donald hissed.

"Then why are you whispering?" Churchill smiled.

Suddenly the ship's search light was turned on and the two men were blinded, then Calloway swerved it away and their eyes counted four men, only two were armed. Calloway's hands were on the light and I looked away in the shame of a traitor. Renda lazily held his gun like a cowboy who knew he could outdraw anyone, only Kondarkov was ready, like a dog straining at it's leash. "Good morning gentlemen," Renda laughed.

Now Donald found his courage again and stepped forwards, "you know why we are here, now give us the child."

"Now why would we do that?" Renda mocked.

"Because I will kill you otherwise you bloody Yank," Donald replied.

Renda knew that he meant it but still grinned, "and I will kill you."
"My life is over anyway, how about yours?" Donald growled.

"Put the gun down Mr Pembridge," Renda spoke to him as if he was a child, "you are clearly outgunned here."

"How do you work that out? It is equal here, two against two," Donald replied.

"I can only see one beneath me," Renda laughed.

"Two!" Donald spat back, "I have Mr Churchill with me."

"Yes I know," Renda repied.

"Then that makes two!"

'No," Renda slowly explained, "that makes three to us."

Donald then turned to Churchill and looked down the barrel of his gun,;his eyes were as hard as when he had faced the Boer. Donald frowned and then his mouth opened but whatever he was going to say was buried beneath thunder as the greatest ever Briton squeezed the trigger. The shot thundred over the water to the Wirral and Donald was blown back dead. Churchill then lowered his gun and looked at his victim, "as he said his life was over anyway."

I staggered back as I recognized a face from the newspapers, "but, but you're Winston Churchill."

Churchill then turned and for a while his face was a murderous cold before it cracked in a smile, "who is this idiot?" The others laughed even Kondrakov.

Renda stepped forwards, "it's Simmonds, he's the one who brought the child to us."

Churchill looked at me, unimpressed but grunted, "then I guess he can be trusted then."

Renda walked forwards and smiled as he looked down at the dead man, before his eyes flitted up to Churchill with a smerk, "is this the biggest one you ever bagged?"

Churchill looked down at the man he had been talking to for four hours or so before without emotion, "yes, you may be right."

"Why did you do that?" I gasped.

Renda then shouted back to Kondrakov, "you'll have to help us with this one, this man is a giant."

"Why did you do that?" I repeated, "you're Winston Churchill."

The statesman's eyes then rose up to me, "My father was British. My mother American, so I can choose and I am choosing America."

"But why?"

"Because the Americans didn't hang me out to dry during the war because of one mistake and send me to the trenches," he replied bitterly

Kondrakov strode down and then Calloway paced down with a stride which said that he hoped it was all over before he got there, together they grabbed Donald's shoulders while Rena and Churchill got his legs and they carried him up the gangplank before dumping him on the deck like a crate of rotten fruit. Churchill picked up an oily rag and cleaned his hands on it as if Donald had died of the plague, he then looked up at Renda, "wait until you are out at sea and then throw him overboard. Pity this isn't South Africa, the sharks would do the job of getting rid of the evidence for you."

"Don't worry," Renda replied, "they'll never find him."

Churchill looked at him, of course he never liked him no one ever likedRenda, but they did what he said and that's all he was worried about, "so I guess that this is the last time that we will see eachother this side of the ocean."

Renda nodded, "yes, this will make me; with this baby we have hit the jackpot."

"It's a shame that I cannot take my share of the credit," Churchill grumbled, "you will have to take it all."

Renda laughed, knowing that Churchill was always his own greatest self publicist."I know that that must kill you."

Churchill looked at Donald's dead face, "you know that was my first Briton, I have shot loads of Boers and Germans but never one of *them* before."

"But you're Winston Churchill," I stammered.

"I'd best go else he is going to say that all night," Churchill laughed.

I watched him walk back down the gangplank and up the muddy track. I heard him mock his driver, calling him a coward; he was no coward, just no killer like us. I saw the car headlamps come on and then drive off into darkness on that long, lonely road we had come up. Calloway disappeared and the ship's engines bellowed out smoke and then it edged slowly up the Flintshire coast, past other vessels which would never leave this place. We were past Wales, past Ireland and in the open ocean when they threw Donald overboard, weighed down by rocks, he had been beginning to let off a stench, and so that was the funeral of the last Lord of Holt Castle.

Epilogue:

Well that was all twenty years ago. My life since has been uneventful, the CIA found no use for me, or maybe they wanted to keep me safe. They have left us alone, but not one day has passed when I haven't noticed someone loitering in the street outside. Maybe they give the job to new people, because they all seem like college kids. I've had the same kind of dead end jobs as I had back home, but I needn't work really, they are still paying us. Don't ask me how we ended up in Los Angeles, we must have lived in a dozen places, this I feel will be the last one.

My first wife gets an allowance, a man from the American embassy use to bring it to her, she ended up marrying him, I'll say one thing for her she never misses an opportunity, and they are living here in the States somewhere. My son is a man now, his problems seem to have passed, that yearning for him has never left me and when I cry, I cry over him. I did ask the CIA to at least let me drive past their house one day so I can see him, but they never give me a reply. I have never met my mother in law but she is still in Rochester, and moved to a house that is faraway from the Medway's floodings thanks to Uncle Sam.

Matilda and I had two girls, baby sisters to the one we saved from the evil English. She is a woman now, we told her who she *was*; we had to too many people told her who she looked like. She went peroxide and those comments ended, she is a beautiful, intelligent and caring young woman, she would have made the British a wonderful princess, but their loss has been our gain. We never had another son, so both Matilda and I yearn for the ones we lost.

Holt Castle itself still stands there and I have noticed that it has started to appear on maps, marked as a historic building, without explanation as to why it wasn't there before. Mrs Fitzroy died, The CIA told me that the Tasman wolves pulled her apart, it was her husband who they respected he was the only one saving her from them, one night she tried to shepherd them into their pen and they rounded on her, her head disappeared into their leader's mouth and he tore it off like uprroting a pumpkin. The wolves themselves disappeared, if you look them up in the enclyopdeia britannica it will say that the last one died in Hobart zoo in 1936.

There is an old map of Essex on my wall, and a few pictures of East Ham, and a portrait of Anne Boleyn, Kondrakov was right about that, it is nice to have a little shrine to your homeland, especially here in this soulless city. I was proud to British in 1914 I certainly was. Ah what it was to be British back then, to know that you were the best, to see the map with all the pink parts on it as proof, then to be herded up in thousands by your own people and sent to a certain death. It was a murder every bit as hateful as the Armenians who were burnt alive in the Kurdish caves. There I go again, back to talking about the war, even now in 1950.

I will hide this, where I said underneath the floorboards, and I hope this place doesn't have mice, but then Los Angeles doesn't seem to have any wildlife, no mice, no insects nothing. The reader will now say that there were scenes that I couldn't have known, because neither I or my wife were there, well I am a writer, and writers need an imagination at times. If you don't believe in any of this so be it.

If the CIA are reading this, thanks, thanks for giving us a fairly normal life.

If my people back home are reading this, no doubt you are calling me a traitor. Let me tell you this two figures stand out in the American War of Independence, George Washinton was a rebel who took up arms against the British and Benedict Arnold stood by his king and country, guess who has a statue in London?

Charles Simmonds November 15[th 1950], West Beverley, Los Angeles, California.

Epilogue II:

This document was found beneath the floor boards of a West Beverley apartment by John Fowler, on March 26th 1992, there was a scrap of paper also found which seems to be in connection with it: It seems to be a speech no doubt by Fitzroy but we can't be certain:"We were the last line of defense against the Welsh bandits. There was a ditch dug in good King Offa's day, and the Mercians dug it deep but they kept picking at it like rats trying to get into a pantry, and once they found their way through they came east, sweeping over the shires of Hereford, Shropshire and Worcester's shire, then only the river stood between them and the soft pastures of middle England. Castles like Holt stood as Jerichos against the Welsh plague, our ancestors rode out from your castle to stop them crossing the river.They have been back since then, Glendower himself came with his army filled with Welsh and French bandits came and attacked Worcester itself! They stole everything they could out of it, in that old Welsh way of theirs and then set the faithful city alight. No, Welsh people can't be trusted."

I would like to dedicate this book to Howard Brown former undefeated and undisputed kickboxing champion who more than that a great guy who I once had the honour to work with.

I would not like to thank my father, brother and wife for their help with this workl. I would be proud if I had a son, brother or spouse who wrote books, but I guess we are all different.

The pictures are:

Charles Simmonds posing? at the Los Angeles river 1950. Holt Castle. Holt Church. Dunstall Castle. One of Fitzroy's Tasman Wolves. Worcester Gaol. Holt Fleet. Abberley Clock Tower. Worcester cathedral. Grimley brick pits. Winston Churchill. Flint Castle.

THE END

16508504R00088

Printed in Great Britain
by Amazon